The Birthright
of Mary
Magdalene

JOAN RIISE

BALBOA
PRESS

A DIVISION OF HAY HOUSE

The Scripture quotations contained herein are from the New Revised Standard Version Bible, copyright © 1989, Division of Christian Education of the National Council of the Churches of Christ in the United States of America. Used by permission. All rights reserved.

Balboa Press books may be ordered through booksellers or by contacting:

Balboa Press
A Division of Hay House
1663 Liberty Drive
Bloomington, IN 47403
www.balboapress.com
1 (877) 407-4847

Because of the dynamic nature of the Internet, any web addresses or links contained in this book may have changed since publication and may no longer be valid. The views expressed in this work are solely those of the author and do not necessarily reflect the views of the publisher, and the publisher hereby disclaims any responsibility for them.

The author of this book does not dispense medical advice or prescribe the use of any technique as a form of treatment for physical, emotional, or medical problems without the advice of a physician, either directly or indirectly. The intent of the author is only to offer information of a general nature to help you in your quest for emotional and spiritual well-being. In the event you use any of the information in this book for yourself, which is your constitutional right, the author and the publisher assume no responsibility for your actions.

Any people depicted in stock imagery provided by Thinkstock are models, and such images are being used for illustrative purposes only. Certain stock imagery © Thinkstock.

Print information available on the last page.

ISBN: 978-1-5043-3844-8 (sc)
ISBN: 978-1-5043-3845-5 (e)

Balboa Press rev. date: 8/31/2015

The Lord created me at the beginning of his work,
the first of his acts of long ago.
Ages ago I was set up, at the first,
before the beginning of the earth.
When he established the heavens, I was there,
when he drew a circle on the face of the deep,
then I was beside him, like a master worker;
and I was daily his delight,
rejoicing before him always.
(Proverbs 8:22-23, 27, 30)

Come to me, you who desire me, and eat your fill of my fruits.
For the memory of me is sweeter than honey,
and the possession of me sweeter than the honeycomb.
(Sirach 24: 19-20)

Dedication

Grandmothers Frieda and Minnie Jewel
Mother Muriel · Daughter Shanti
Granddaughter Riise
All Sisters in Spirit

Foreword

Who was Mary Magdalene? Where did she come from? What made her the unforgettable and fearless woman of her time, a lightning rod for both divine energy and popular scorn?

In an effort to discover the essence of Mary, the idea occurred to seek her going backwards. What cultural roots, values, spiritual beliefs and philosophical ideals might have influenced her development?

So, here we meet the seven year old Mary as she is about to embark upon the journey to Bethlehem with her mother and grandmother, midwives to Mary of Nazareth. On evenings around the campfires, *herstory* is told through the voice of her grandmother, Sakinah.

As someone who has sought spiritual resonance among the world's religions, it's interesting at this point in my life that I've been drawn back to my own roots. Educated in the Catholic schools of the 50's and 60's, Mary Magdalene was a heroine of mythic proportions. Before recognition and forgiveness, she was the Bad Girl of the Bible — misunderstood, denied, distorted, nearly stoned for following her heart - fascinating stuff for a teen on the brink of women's liberation and the era of free love.

Mary has stayed at the top of my list as I've watched her transform from harlot, to equal partner in divine mission,

Apostle to the Apostles, the woman who sparked heresies. Through it all, she's maintained her radiance even as she has continued to intrigue.

There are already so many myths, legends and books about Mary Magdalene. Need there be more? And yet the story in my head demanded a voice. I researched and generally followed the interwoven strands of Biblical and secular history. She became real as I allowed free rein for dreams and imagination to direct the writing. The characters took on a life of their own leading the way down paths I hadn't anticipated. My own wonder grew as I realized I am myself a seeker and that much is learned through the process of listening in the silence.

Seven. A mystical number associated with creation, perfection, spiritual awakening and esoteric understanding. At seven, Mary is at the stage of development where she is moving beyond her own self-absorption. She is smart, sweet, eager, open to life, insatiably curious, an original. She listens, enthralled by Sakinah's stories; these are, after all, her own stories going back seven generations. The courage, creativity, independence and wisdom learned through their telling are indeed, her birthright.

It is my hope that this story resonates with women; that young women in particular may find relevance and strength as well as liberation from cultural strictures that are still imposed upon us millennia removed from the time of its telling.

Blessed be.

The widow walked the dusty footpath with a grace that belied her age. Her pace quickened as she neared her destination - Magdala.

The tower city shimmered in the late afternoon sunlight, reflecting the Sea of Galilee in all its bustle, beauty and diversity. Soon she would be at her daughter's door. Soon she would be with her granddaughter, Mary.

Though she was clothed in widow's black, her presence and gait intimated far more than a shadow of misfortune. She emanated the light of joy and a confidence earned through life's experience.

Sakinah had been widowed as a young mother. She raised her only child Hannah alone making a life for them both as midwife and healer. Her husband was a fisherman when he was killed, thrown from his boat in a sudden tumult of the sea. They had both grown up in Capernaum, she learning the healing uses of native plants and roots, the making of poultices, salves, teas and potions from her mother; he following in the trade of his father. Fisherman and midwife, she and her husband were woven deeply into the fabric of community, both trusted and respected. Upon his death she chose to remain in Capernaum, content to grow in her healing knowledge and to raise her child while assisting others into the world. She remembered attending births as a little girl, just about the same age Mary was now.

She neared the garden gate that surrounded Hannah's family home. Sakinah entered passing under the grape vines that hung heavy with clusters around the archway. She smiled at Hannah's sign posted on the inner door leading to the beeyard - I WORK FOR THE QUEEN - but before she could even enter she was mugged from behind with a joyful squeal, "Nana! You're here! Guess who's hugging you right now! I am *so* happy!" Sakinah turned to scoop Mary up in her arms hugging her close to her heart.

At almost seven, Mary was a lightning bolt of energy, articulate for one so young; she was a beautiful child with hair the color of honey inherited from the generations of women before her. Her blue eyes flecked with gold, held a deep animation of spirit. She was small of build but powerful and she expressed an intelligence far beyond such few years.

"Mary! I've missed you so much! I'm here for a visit and to join you on our trip to Bethlehem."

"We're going on a trip? I've never been to Bethlehem, have I? Does Mama know? Let's go tell her! She's with her bees." After first helping Mary into a protective head covering and then her own, they entered the bee yard. They found Hannah sitting quietly across from her hives.

"Mother! Welcome!" Arms wide, Hannah rose quickly opening to a warm embrace that included the child, Mary. I'm so glad you're here! I was just thinking of all that needs to be done in preparation for our trip.

Mary and I are just back ourselves from a visit with Mary and Joseph in Nazareth. They're so glad you'll be traveling with us - two midwives in attendance ensure a peaceful birth. They are grateful for your years of experience and I *always* welcome your presence."

"Mama! I didn't know we were going on a trip. Together with Nanny... I'm so excited!"

"I didn't want to tell you, Mary, until our plans were settled. I know you're excited! This will be your first real journey. We'll be on the road traveling for at least week or more. The most special surprise is that you'll be with us as we attend to Mary for what likely will be time for the birth of her baby. After all our visits together, Mary and Joseph have come to love you. They consider you a big girl and even though you're still my *little* girl, your Nana believes you're the right age to begin helping. She was as old as you are now when her Mama began bringing her along."

"Oh, Mama! Nana! Just imagine! I don't know what to think!"

"Mary, we'll be with you the whole time. Mostly you'll learn from watching and listening but sometimes we might ask you to do something simple like bring water, light or sweet oil. Birth is a miracle, each one so different. Even your Nana and I never know quite what to expect. Mary of Nazareth is young and strong, anticipating this birth with great love and Joseph is so kind. Although it would be nice for her to deliver in her own home, this trip is commanded by Caesar Augustus. Though we're not of the House of David, we accompany Mary to assist the birth of her child."

Turning to Sakinah, Hannah continued, "Mother! You must be tired and hungry after your long walk. Let's leave the bees buzzing and move into the house so you can refresh and I can begin preparing our supper."

"And Mary," Sakinah promised, "this trip will give us lots of time for stories; stories I shared with your Mama when she was little; stories about our grandmothers. Come, help your old Nana with my bags and I'll show you some of the special things I bring for the birthing." Sakinah and Mary went off together while Hannah began preparations for the evening meal.

"Along with you now, child! Your papa will be home soon and he'll be hungry. Go help your grandmother with whatever she needs. Bring her a pitcher of water and a basin to wash. When you finish with Nana, come help me and we'll light the candles for supper. We'll enjoy this easy time together before our journey."

Ari came home from the wharf carrying the main course for the evening's meal. Kissing Hannah on the neck as he entered, Ari added vibrant male energy along with the fresh scent of the sea to the household ruled by his queens. "Delicious, no? Where is my dancing princess and the dowager queen? It was a good day and I love you all! I'm so glad Sakinah will be making this journey with you. Joseph will take good care of Mary and her two renowned midwives! I'm sure he would rather not be traveling so close to Mary's delivering but with you and Sakinah along it will assure him peace of mind at least. And welcoming Mary as well! What does she think of this now that she knows?"

Their conversation was interrupted by Mary's clattering down the stairs ahead of her grandmother. "Papa! You're home! Guess what! Mama, Nana and I are going on a trip to Bethlehem and I'm going to be a midwife! Nana says so and Mary and Joseph think I'm a big girl!"

Sakinah, laughing at Mary's breathless news, came forward and opened her arms to Ari. "Greetings, my son! I'm glad to see you looking so well. It's good to be here with you. Thank you for your gracious hospitality."

Ari embraced his mother-in-law with deep affection then stepped back to bow in welcome and respect for her life's work.

Smiling, Hannah stepped close and kissing her excited daughter on the top of her head whispered, "Mary! Close your eyes a moment, stand still through three deep breaths, then don't say a word until dinner. I need you to help me. This is good practice. Yes, you will be our big girl apprentice and helper. You will learn best by listening and taking what you see and hear into your heart to understand. It is in silence that you will learn all you need to know. *Nous**?" Mary settled immediately. A look of acknowledgement went between Sakinah and her daughter.

The evening became focused as supper was prepared. Candles were lit and Hannah decorated the table with hyssop and lavender, favorite flowers of the honey bees. She brought out a bottle of her honey wine and taking each other's hands in a circle around the table, they began the evening meal with a blessing of grace and gratitude.

---

* *Nous – awareness of a deeper knowing; beneath the surface; spiritual perception*

Later, as dishes were cleared Sakinah and Hannah found themselves alone. "So Mary understands the *nous,* my daughter?"

"Mother, she expressed her understanding one day while we were sitting with the bees. Though she didn't know the word *nous,* she told me she knows things about them because they speak to her heart. Words aren't necessary for her to understand, she says. She comprehends the essence of their lives and the healing they can bring to those in need. She's young but already I can sense the woman she will be. I'm glad for this coming journey and the time it will afford us to be together so you can share our stories. That Joseph and Mary are so kind and interested in her stills any concerns I might have about her presence at the birth."

"Ah, Hannah, daughter of my heart! You too are wise for your years. The path for women is not easy. I am grateful for the wisdom of our foremothers. They've passed to us the history, mystery and artistry of life. There's joy in their stories as well as sorrow; courage, passion, imagination, beauty, faith, strength and perseverance, all qualities of character that led them onward even through the darkest times. Mary may be young but she's ready.

"I'm glad also, for the love you share with Ari, my lion of a son-in-law. He is life's blessing bestowed upon you and Mary. He cherishes not only your beauty but your fearlessness, compassion and contribution to life itself. Not a day goes by that I don't remember your beloved father, Baruch. You and I have much to be grateful for; life flows best when there is balance. Like your father, Ari respects and honors your life's work. Blessed be the strength and memory of Baruch and the understanding and equanimity of your husband Ari."

Early the following morning, Mary helped Sakinah carry down and load her birthing supplies: salves of honey, beeswax and oil of almonds, poultices of propolis, healing herbs and clay, lavender and hyssop to sweeten the birthing bed and several goatskins of Hannah's legendary honey wine. With Ari's blessing, the women and child began their journey. They traveled first to Nazareth where, in a few days, they would join others on the caravan to Bethlehem with Mary and Joseph. Concerned for her safety through the arduous trip, Joseph had insisted on a donkey so Mary could ride with less chance of exhaustion. For reasons of weather, terrain and avoiding bandits, it had been decided to take the longer route down to Jericho and then up through the Judean Desert to Jerusalem and Bethlehem. Typically a caravan could cover 20 miles a day but with a woman nine months pregnant, the trip demanded patience and good sense.

The weather was far from dependable at that time of year - pleasant during the day with temperatures dropping at night. After a long day of travel, tents were raised, fires built and welcome food prepared. It was around the nightly fire that Mary, snuggled warmly against her grandmother's breast, began to hear the tales of her foremothers.

"Let me begin Mary, by saying how blessed I am to share these stories with you. They are accounts that belong to all the women of our family, even to the daughters you may bring into the world. There is good reason to know your past. You'll find wisdom and guidance in these stories so you never feel alone. From each of them you can glean a value that will lend meaning and confidence to the choices you make in your own life. You are young but already your bees have helped you understand that there is more to life than what you know through your senses. There is an inner voice that you learn to hear in stillness; it opens a deeper knowing of truth. We call this the *nous,* and from what your mother tells me, the bees are your teachers and you have already begun to understand."

"Oh, yes, Nana! The Queen tells me how they are here from the beginning of time, to aid us in healthy living. She has taught me never to fear them, that they are gentle and mean no harm. Her daughters sting only when they feel threatened. It saddens her to lose even one through their bravery in her defense, for it means sure death to that one. She's also told me that there are good things that can come even if I am stung by accident but I hope that doesn't happen anytime soon, I know it hurts."

Sakinah smiled. "She teaches you well, my child and you are eager to learn. The bees open the door for you to the mystery of life. It's like the Sea of Galilee. Where would we be if we knew water only from its surface? Truth is discovered in silence, beyond the senses and in the depth beneath the surface.

"Your life, sweet Mary, is a gift. You are blessed with a loving family. Through the stories you'll gain insight and courage, determination to persevere even through the challenges and sorrows life may have in store for you. No one knows the future but a foundation built on love, with respect for life in all its diversity, and appreciation of your own family history — all this will serve you well."

Sakinah could feel the nodding of Mary's head. Savoring the closeness of their bodies, Sakinah sighed, "Sleep deep, dear child and dream. Your Mama and I are here. May the angels watch over you this night."

The new day dawned clear with just a lingering of the season's warmth. Mary's excitement was boundless as they walked new paths, scenery changing even in a day. She questioned unfamiliar birds, trees, plants, flowers and scents upon the wind; from the clouds she imagined stories of her own, and with the innocence of the child she was, she brought smiles to travelers growing weary, inspiring each to reserves of energy they didn't realize they possessed.

Mary and Joseph welcomed her company, Joseph often lifting her to ride along with Mary on the donkey. Together the two Marys would sing the songs of childhood, enchanting all who walked close by with the sweetness of their voices. On occasion, the donkey's rhythmic gait would lull the two to sleep, each supported by the other as they rode. Joseph felt his spirit calm, his heart filled with gratitude at the unexpected love blossoming between the two Marys. He led them forward with renewed confidence and faith.

That night after assisting the women in the chores of clean-up, Mary came to rest at last with Hannah and Sakinah as they sat around the fire circle. Together they acknowledged all that she was learning. Any doubt her elders might have held that Mary was too young for such an experience had disappeared. In so many ways, Mary was a natural with a heightened sensitivity to her surroundings. She welcomed new ideas and people with the magnetic attraction of bees to pollen.

"Nana! Are you going to begin telling me the stories tonight? Since I already know all about you and Mama, will you go back to the beginning; as *far* back as you can remember. Please!"

"Ah, good! Yes, it's right to begin at the beginning for any story, but you must know, Mary, that there is much before a time that even I cannot remember. Stories are handed down mother to daughter around the fire as we are now, in the Moon Chamber you'll come to know, and during our *mikvahs* – our ritual purification baths.

"Life sometimes presents challenges that prevent the handing down of stories from one mother to the next, one generation to the next. It doesn't take long before the tale is altered or forgotten altogether. Let this journey we three travel be your initiation ritual to the element of fire. Perhaps what you hear will spark a devotion to developing the character and values that will guide and empower your own life.

"Each of us has a purpose in life. For your mother and me, it's been tending the bees and bringing new life into the world; sacred tasks, indeed. From *my* mother Sofia, I learned the art and skills of caring for bees that she brought to Galilee from Egypt. But since we'll begin at the beginning, I'll leave her story until the end and begin tomorrow night with Epona."

Attentive, Mary quickly piped up, "I thought we were beginning tonight!"

Putting her hand gently on top of Mary's, Hannah suggested quietly, "Think about it, Mary... all you've been learning already. Think about how the bees come home to their hive each evening laden with pollen and nectar. Though pollen is the *nugget* of the sweetness to come, it needs the *process* of the hive to transform it into honey. Don't you think it might be a good idea tonight for you to *absorb* all of today in your dreams so you can better understand?

"As you consider all that Mary, Nana and I thought of a special project for you. To signify the importance of this journey, we'll help you create your own walking staff. Tomorrow morning as the sun comes up, before breaking fast, Nana will take you away from camp. Together you'll look for a tree limb big enough it will serve you as you grow and carry you forward as you walk many roads."

Thoughtful, Mary quickly posited, "I want my staff to represent the pathway of my life. I want to mark it in some way so that it will remind me of everything I learn along the way.

"Nana! Mama! I know you'll want to help me! Tomorrow, Nana, we will find the strongest, most beautiful tree limb in the whole world! It will be from a tree that flowers in the spring; a tree whose nectar draws the bees. It will be just the right size to be useful to me now and even as I grow. It will smell good too; I'll hang ribbons and gourds and stones with hearts that I find along the way. It will be a map of the journey of my life and when my own life is over, the staff will continue to provide support for *my* daughters and granddaughters!

"Since you suggest this task is an initiation of fire, will the signs be made in the heat of the flames? Then surely that's where I need your help so I don't burn too much or too little, or even burn myself! I want each picture to help me remember."

Hannah hugged her daughter close, impressed with how completely she'd grasped the project. "Have no fear! We'll teach you symbols that in just a stroke or two will contain the whole story in a nutshell making it easy for you to remember."

Sakinah and Hannah smiled together at the innocence and fullness of Mary's expression. A wave of imagination moved across her face like a wind reflecting the dancing flames before her. Looking into the eyes of each beloved, Mary admitted, "You're right Mama, Nana. I have so much to put together in my head. I think I will sleep now; it will be time to be up before I know it. Tomorrow I find my staff! Thank you Mama! Thank you, Nana!"

Hannah and her mother chimed in chorus, "May the angels watch over you this night, sweet daughter. Sleep in peace."

Birdsong riffed with an edge of excitement in the dark just before dawn. Mary lay awake beside her grandmother listening as the sweetness of their song harkened her to the day. Breathing deeply in anticipation, she felt the gentle touch of Sakinah's hand nudging her to dress silently then venture with her away from camp. A scent and sound so familiar floated towards them as Mary recognized the contented buzz of bees sipping their morning nectar.

Sakinah knew what they would find just beyond the circle of camp. At dusk of the previous day she'd seen the almond grove and knew that among its branching trunks they'd find the perfect limb for Mary's staff. Together they stood in wonder as the sun barely lifted over the horizon shedding its arcing rays of purple, pink and blue, winding gracefully through the grove, illuminating the beauty of almond trees blooming in their fullness. The moon and Venus still hung in the sky as night turned to day.

They walked quietly, senses alive in the dawning light. Tree limbs were scattered here and there where earlier pruning had dropped them to the ground. Mary grew excited as she moved among the trees, picking up likely prospects, judging them on Sakinah's advice, for sturdiness, length, weight, scent, and how a curve, crook or knot might feel in her hand as she grew taller. Momentarily they were drawn to a particular tree, slightly apart from the others, appearing larger and older than the rest.

"A *Mother Tree!*" Sakinah whispered with reverence. A crescendo of buzzing revealed a hive of feral bees clustered tightly among her branches, their heavy comb apparent through the branches. She led Mary forward with respect and the easy assurance that their search was over.

"Nana, here, look! I've found it! It's perfect! It's as tall as Mama so there's lots of room to grow. See the crook at the top? I can hang a gourd for water as I walk; there's even a knothole beneath where I can tie ribbons and holey stones! Look at this little curve under the crook and then see how it straightens out, so strong all the way to the ground."

Sakinah smiled acknowledging Mary's perfect find. "You are blessed, little Mary, with a gift from the Queen of Heaven herself! Your bees called you right to it. It would be a good idea, don't you think, to give thanks in some small way?"

"Oh, yes, Nana!" From her pocket, Mary pulled out a small stone in the shape of a heart that she'd picked up on the first day of their journey. Kneeling at the trunk of the tree, she dug a little hole with her hands in the soft dirt between roots. *"Dear Mother Tree; Sweet Queen Bee!* Thank you for this beautiful limb that over time will assist me as I walk down the roads of my life. Nana and Mama will help me with the symbols along its length so that I'll never forget my stories. With their blessing and yours, I will venture bravely on many journeys; this branch will tell it all. Please accept this little heart as a symbol of my thanks for the gift you have given."

With that, Mary covered the stone with earth, kissed the ground and patting the trunk affectionately she stood, already lifting herself with the aid of her staff. She beamed at her grandmother with a smile of innocence, accomplishment and delight. "Come! Let's go show Mama; she needs to see this!"

Hannah welcomed them back, already finished with the morning's preparation for departure. She listened to Mary's joyful telling of her discovery, especially appreciating the role played by the bees. Throughout the day's walk, Mary asked questions of how, why and what, sometimes offering sparks of insight as understanding grew.

Though her walking staff was far longer than her own height, she carried it with pride, imagining the travels through which it might carry her. She stayed close to Mary and Joseph, sharing in depth the wonder and intention of her discovery along with the gift she'd left behind. As shadows lengthened but miles yet remained in the day's trek, Joseph recognized her waning energy. Without objection, he lifted her up to open arms where she nestled into Mary's warmth and quickly fell asleep. Smiling, Joseph gently removed the staff from her tight-fisted little hand and tied it securely against the animal's flank. Mary hummed a lullaby. Catching his wife's contented glance, they smiled together. "Good practice!" Joseph suggested as he led his precious cargo forward.

Hannah and Sakinah, never far from the pregnant couple, watched the tender vignette as it evolved. Hannah whispered to her mother, "It seems my Mary holds a special place in their hearts."

By late afternoon the travelers halted for the day. Tents were pitched, wood gathered and fires set against the chill of coming night. After three days on the journey everyone was accustomed to the rhythm and routine of the daily pace. Less fatigued, the general camaraderie became tangible. People moved around camp easily, sharing insights from the day's experience. Mothers clustered around Mary and Joseph eager to tell tales of their own births. With so many attentive women surrounding her, Joseph was able to move off quietly to enjoy companionship among the men.

Hannah, Sakinah and Mary were in deep conversation as they considered the first symbol to be burned onto the base of the staff. Mary was clear, "I want my first to be a heart because my own heart is so full for such a gift and all that I am learning on this trip."

"That's a lovely idea, Mary. Your journey begins in love. Now let me show you how we do this." Sakinah reached for a length of sturdy kindling. She put the tip into the flames waiting until it glowed. Pulling it out, she rolled it in the dirt then thrust it back again into the fire. When the tip was once more a glowing ember, she removed it, rolling it around then back into the flames. She did this over and over until the tip was as sharp as a stylus. "Watch now, Mary. See how red hot and sharp I've made the tip. Now it's ready and we can burn the heart into the base of the staff." Ever so carefully, with Mary kneeling close to see, Sakinah burned the mark. "There, Mary! And so your story begins!"

Sitting back on her heels, Sakinah looked with love into Mary's eyes and those of her own daughter who had missed nothing of the moment. "May you always find the blessings of love, truth and courage along the way."

Mary bowed her head as she accepted her grandmother's blessing. Taking hold of the staff she raised herself to standing, feet planted firmly. Solemnly she said, "Thank you, Nana. Thank you, Mama. Now I know." Hannah and Sakinah embraced the child with deep emotion. They stood together in silence under the stars, aware of the portent of the moment.

"Well, now! It certainly seems to me that tonight is a good time to begin. Let's all get comfortable around the fire. There will be much you don't understand but let me tell the story in the rhythm in which it was told to me. When I'm finished you can ask questions." In a moment, Mary was snuggled against her mother's heart, alert and eager.

"It begins many generations past in a land far to the north and west. The people there moved on horseback across a terrain of grasslands and savannas. Their way of life was determined by the women of the tribe. Women owned property. Talent directed their life's work, some choosing to tend crops and animals, or to become artisans or midwives. There were even women warriors who were legendary for their fierceness. Women decided who and even if they would marry. Justice and order were maintained by a council of wise women and elders. Because women give birth they were respected as givers of life and the Great Mother was central to everything alive: people, animals, birds and fish, water, weather, crops, trees, flowers, vegetables and bees — *everything*!

"Epona, daughter of Canan and granddaughter of Freyda, lived a spirited life; she also had a twin brother named Azad. From the time Epona was a small child no older than you, Mary, she had a way with horses; her name in fact, means *protector of horses*. Epona was fearless! As soon as her mother carried her near, the horses would whinny their welcome. She learned to walk among their legs, pulling herself to standing by grabbing their tails. As a toddler she was already riding bareback.

"As they grew older, she and Azad became acrobats on the backs of their galloping mounts. Epona danced as if she were a part of the horse, gracefully lifting her arms like a bird in flight, balancing first on one leg then spinning to another. Azad equaled her skill as he mastered flips and handstands. With ultimate patience, Epona could gentle a wild stallion by standing still, meeting his gaze until he came to her, head bowed in surrender. With her mother and grandmother she learned to assist laboring mares deliver their foals as she grew in confidence and skill. Azad shared her passion; horses were their life! Together they tasted freedom, galloping like the wind across broad, open ranges far from home but always returning in time for the evening meal with wondrous tales to tell. Epona and Azad grew in beauty, strength and curiosity as each day became a grand discovery. Because the twins were always together Freyda and Canan were never afraid for their safety.

"In the little history I know of Freyda, their grandmother, she had come to this land as a young child from a country far to the north. She arrived with her father, Norman, a widowed merchant traveling the Roman route with carts laden full of rare goods. There he met the beautiful Behar, a Seer of far vision who had long awaited their arrival. Behar healed his grief, opening his heart again to a springtime of love; Freyda she embraced with a mother's love.

"Freyda took to the life of the horse like bees to nectar. It has been passed down through generations since, that it was from Freyda that the women of our family inherit our golden, honey colored hair and the sky blue of our eyes. Freyda attracted suitors from far and wide perhaps because her coloring set her apart from the darker complexioned members of the tribe. She chose well and it came to pass, from the deeply rooted union of Alon and Freyda that Canan, their beloved daughter was born. In the next generation then it was from the union of Canan and Karim that the twins, Epona and Azad were born.

"With such heritage in their blood it was no surprise to Freyda or her daughter that an urge to explore should overtake the twins as they grew to be adults. Out of respect and love for their mother and grandmother they came one day to share their restlessness and desire to experience life beyond the steppes. They'd already discovered in their forays away from camp, the Roman roads and caravans moving in all directions. On numerous occasions they'd had opportunity to talk with merchants, travelers, craftsmen and soldiers. Sometimes they had only the language of sign to communicate but quick to learn, they'd easily begun picking up words and concepts from people of many nations. They learned that their experience and talent with horses could be put to good use. Together they could tame, train and minister to any horse that might come their way.

"Among the many tales of distant lands, it was the majesty of Greece that beckoned; Greece with its great centers of commerce, art, learning and culture. With the blessing of their mother and grandmother, they would leave with the next caravan moving in that direction.

"Freyda and Canan knew there would be no stopping them. They expressed concern only for Epona's safety for she was of marriage age and beautiful. They encouraged the twins to consider their objection and to think it over carefully before rushing ahead. Headstrong and sure, Epona cut off her flowing hair and came back to them the following morning dressed as a male in her brother's clothing. 'Now I will have not only the protection of my strong brother Azad, but I will go forth confidently as his twin brother! On any horse I am swift and clever enough to avoid danger without violence.'

"Any objections were thus stunned into silence and so it was agreed that, trading upon their skill with horses and with the blessing of both Freyda and Canan, they would embark upon their journey as soon as all was in readiness. In the time left together, they assembled supplies - tents, bedding, food and a surplus of tack for their horses; besides their two favorites, they decided to bring several additional horses to carry gear and for possible trade along the way. Anticipation and preparation kept their minds focused, time passed quickly. At the last it was their youthful bravado that finally set them on their path; though the draw was magnetic and their decision clear, they left with tears, not knowing for sure if they would ever meet again."

Sakinah stood to stretch her legs. Mary and Hannah followed her lead. "Nana, I have questions. Is this a good time now?"

"Tell me what you're thinking, child."

"The *Great* Mother, why is she called great?"

"The Mother is great because it is from her that all blessings flow. The people honored her by living in harmony with all of nature. Responsibility was shared equally among men and women. Peace and justice were maintained through a council that listened with open mind to people's concerns. Based on their talents, girls learned trades just like boys to give meaning to their lives and to provide balanced support in their families. There was time and place for rituals of passage, marking the seasons and milestones of life, rituals of appeal for planting, harvesting and hunting, for moon cycles, fertility, marriage, birth and death, and always for gratitude."

Pondering deeply all that she had heard, Mary questioned again, "What about the Great Father?"

"Today our people honor Yahweh, the Lord of Abraham."

With childlike simplicity, Mary ventured again, "So... Yahweh is the Great Father and he's married to the Great Mother... or is she his mother?"

"No, child. Yahweh has no mother nor does he have a wife."

"Nana! How can that be? Everyone has a mother! And men have wives who become mothers!"

Hannah joined the conversation, "There are mysteries in life, Mary, that we come to understand or not; that we accept, or not. We make our own choices. During our moon cycles, a time you will come to know, women gather together in a chamber set apart. There, in privacy each month, women share the old ways, keeping alive the ancient wisdom of the Mother Father God. Women are restricted in many ways by the laws of Yahweh but by keeping traditions alive among ourselves and in our families, balance and harmony are maintained. The stories you're hearing, Mary, have been handed down from mother to daughter for generations. Stories are a valued part of your first initiation."

Comprehension began to dawn on Mary's face, "So... some things are secret? Is that because Yahweh is jealous? Doesn't he recognize or honor woman as a carrier of life?" Fear darted across her little face, "Mama! Can you be punished for being a midwife?"

Hannah embraced her daughter in reassurance; smiling, she continued, "No, Mary. In general, no matter how much they love them, men want little to do with laboring women at the time of birth. Midwives are held in deep regard by peasants and kings alike. We minister not only to the mother and the infant but to her spirit and emotions as well. You will be there with us and Mary, as she births her babe. Each birth is different but each is a miracle. I was your age when your grandmother first brought me along. There were things I didn't understand but we'll prepare you so you are not afraid. You will be our special helper. Perhaps we will ask you to bring water, or a blanket, or maybe to sing a lullaby—perhaps some of the songs you and Mary have been singing together. At a certain point, we may even ask you to spend time outside with Joseph. Though men leave the work of birthing to the midwives, they are always in need of support too. You can see how much Joseph loves his wife and is concerned for her safety and comfort."

Thoughtfully pulling herself up to her full height Mary said with confidence, "I understand now. I'm glad to be a big girl and that you trust me to help. I can keep secrets. I love Mary and Joseph too. I want to hear more about everything, Epona and Azad too but I'm *so* tired. Don't be disappointed, Nana! I'll be ready tomorrow so you can continue."

Arm in arm, they moved from the fire's edge to the comfort of their tent and soft bedrolls. Like the big girl she was growing to be, it was Mary who chimed the night's blessing, "May the angels watch over us *all* this night. Sleep in peace, dear ones."

As the band of travelers prepared to depart the following morning, Hannah came upon Mary and Joseph in a heated discussion. Sakinah and Mary were close behind. Joseph stood beside the donkey, face set firmly in contrast to Mary's increasing demand. "Joseph, let me walk! My body feels cramped. I need to feel the earth beneath my feet!"

Stepping close, Sakinah as elder midwife suggested quietly, "Joseph, there are moments when a man's control needs be tempered by a pregnant woman's determination. Though this is Mary's first, what she asks is instinctively wise. She's been riding three days. Muscles necessary for birthing must be exercised. There's no harm in walking. Trust her! She'll let you know when she needs to ride again."

In the face of such assurance, Joseph's face relaxed visibly. From behind her mother, Mary came forward without hesitation to offer her prized staff. "Here, Mary, please use my new walking staff. It will help you over rocky ground and give you balance. Look, Joseph! It fits Mary just right. I still have to grow into it."

Joseph smiled recalling the pride and value Mary placed on her staff and was deeply touched at her sharing. "Then maybe I'll ride for a while myself," he teased but instead he hoisted little Mary up to the donkey's back, allowing her to ride astride by herself. In the afternoon, Mary returned to riding as the child walked alongside with her mother, grandmother and prized staff.

Late in the day, a fine place with water, trees and flat ground was found for setting up the night's camp. Cooking fires were ignited. The pleasant sounds of family life and food preparation echoed through the air energizing everyone after a long day on the road. It seemed to take forever to clean away the bowls and pots and repack them for the following day's departure. Food for breaking fast was always prepared after supper - dates and nuts and flatbread.

"Nana, before you begin the story tonight" Mary said, "I need to add another symbol to my staff."

"Mary! I'm so happy you're thinking deeply on our journey not only of the story but all that you're experiencing as we move along. What is it that needs to be burned this night?"

"It made me so glad that Mary used my staff today as she walked the road. I know it gave her confidence and balance and it seemed to make Joseph really happy too! They are both so nice to me, I never want to forget them.

I made up a new symbol all by myself so that I will always remember our time together."

"Show me, Mary. Can you draw it first in the sand?" Mary picked up a small, pointed stick and kneeling down drew a circle then, in its center, she made a dot. Hannah saw her mother's knowing smile of approval and came close to see what Mary had created.

"Can you tell me what it means to you, Mary?" she asked.

"Mary is the circle because she is so round and full; her baby is the dot in the center. The dot represents the life she carries in the safe circle of her womb. No matter how old I grow to be, I'll always remember her, the babe within and this trip we're making together before he's born." They moved to the fire's edge and carefully burned the second symbol onto the staff. Then, satisfied that the day's work was accomplished, they retired to the warmth of their tent to continue the story.

"So! Epona and Azad were finally on their way. They traveled the Roman's *Via Egnatia* that ran hundreds of miles from their home near Dyrrachium through Macedonia and Greece all the way to Byzantium. Among the travelers were people of color, speaking unfamiliar tongues. The twins adapted easily to using sign language to communicate. There were musicians with stringed instruments, flutes and drums; artisans, weavers and merchants, jugglers and acrobats, story-tellers, soldiers and slaves. Some travelers walked, some rode donkeys, soldiers rode horseback and merchants traveled in carts brimming with precious wares.

"As they grew comfortable with the company, Epona and Azad amazed their neighbors with agile feats of daring on horseback. They learned to juggle and before long added burning torches to their acrobatics. Night time fires were lively and full of new experience. Percussive rhythms brought people to their feet renewing energy even after a long day on the road; string and wind instruments lulled melodies of beauty and reflection.

"Azad was particularly drawn to the artisans of varied skills - jewelry, pottery, carving, veils of gossamer silk, flax and fine linen, soft carpets woven of patterns and spectacular colors he had never seen. He spent many evenings with the merchants, intrigued by a lifestyle that not only appreciated the value of such artistry but that found markets while traveling to exotic locations far and wide.

"On occasion the caravan set-up camp for several days, resting and gathering supplies while the merchants visited the locals, trading treasures and acquiring more. The townspeople were equally drawn to the travelers' camp by the music and story-telling such opportunities provided.

"Azad and Epona performed their horseback feats delighting the crowds that expressed their appreciation by tossing coins, trinkets and bracelets. It wasn't long before Azad realized the purse that was growing as a result of their antics. With Epona in agreement, he embarked upon the acquisition of beautiful, hand-crafted goods, soon venturing into the towns himself, testing his own skills at trading.

"Near Edessa they were joined by a handsome young man riding a magnificent stallion of noble stature and high spirit. The horses drew them together and quickly they learned all about the Arabian breed that set the young man's horse apart from their own.

"They discovered he was returning to Thessaloniki where his father was Master of Horse at the Roman garrison. His name was Chenzira which meant *born on a journey*. He laughed as he told how his Roman father Aquila had fallen in love with a beautiful Egyptian woman named Nofret. They had married, living in Egypt for a time. When Aquila was transferred to Thessaloniki, Nofret was very pregnant but insisted on traveling with her husband. Of course, Chenzira was born along the way! Such a perfect name and he had been living up to it ever since, he told them. The three developed a spirited bond and from that moment were inseparable.

"Though their backgrounds varied greatly, they learned with open minds of each other's way of life, of the Great Mother and of the gods and goddesses that ruled both in Egypt and in Rome. Though she was still known as Azad's brother, Epona questioned Chenzira about the role of women in both societies. She learned that in Egypt women had more opportunity for education and that in daily life they were respected as equals even to the extent of being valued for their opinions in government and religion. Roman women on the other hand, were educated primarily in the arts for the purpose of finding good husbands. Their daily lives were more sequestered than Egyptian women yet, as in many cultures, they ruled their families thereby influencing from behind the scenes, issues important to them. In both cultures women were in control on matters relating to childbirth; midwives and healers were respected although in Greece, the fields of medicine, health and philosophy were dominated by men.

"During days on the road, they often ventured ahead on their own, scouting conditions, locating water, visiting towns, communicating with villagers or lone travelers they met along the way. Azad traded every chance he got; already one of his spare horses was laden with treasure. Enthusiastically, he shared his vision of traveling the world as a merchant trader at the same time that Chenzira urged them both to consider joining him and his family at the garrison in Thessaloniki. As Master of Horse, his father would place high value on their skill not only to train horses but to care for them and assist at their births. Azad admitted that the opportunity to work with the spirited Arabians was a draw nearly equal to his desire for a life of freedom on the road. Epona eagerly voiced her favor for, in fact, she found herself powerfully attracted to Chenzira and was conflicted more and more in her role as Azad's brother. Even before they arrived at their destination, it was decided that if Aquila was in agreement, they would stay.

"After many weeks and hundreds of miles, they all found themselves anticipating their destination. Chenzira wanted to ride ahead to greet his parents and to advance the proposal with his father. He had been away for many months and he knew his mother especially would want time alone to welcome him back. That accomplished, he would return to Epona and Azad so they could ride to the garrison together.

"In two days' time, Chenzira was back with the caravan, excited to share his father's welcome. His mother too was in favor for in Egypt, twins were bringers of good fortune. She respected her son's choices especially as he expressed such high esteem for his new friends.

"As official welcome to his son and friends, Aquila had his cavalry stationed along the road leading to the entrance of the garrison. Sitting tall on their mounts with Chenzira between them, Epona and Azad were aware of the wild beat of their hearts as they approached. Though they'd become acquainted with soldiers along the journey, they had never witnessed the awesome spectacle of a full military display.

"Once through the gates, Chenzira took the lead, guiding them to his parents' lodging where they stood waiting. Nofret came forward, arms open in welcome for her son and his handsome friends. Aquila too moved towards them, interested initially more in their horses than the riders. Appreciating their muscle, health and sturdy build, he then turned his attention the twins, offering his arm in a salute of welcome.

"A little girl with hair as black as night came running down the stairs to her mother peeking shyly around her skirts at the strangers in the courtyard. Diffusing any awkwardness of the moment, Chenzira laughed heartily. Swooping down to pick her up, he swung her high in the air eliciting squeals of delight. 'Meet Nuri, my little *gypsy* of a sister! She's always on the look-out for high mischief! Nuri! Meet my new friends, Epona and Azad. Just wait 'til you see the tricks they can do on horseback. You'll think they are part horse themselves!'

'Father, I know you want to show Epona and Azad the quarters where they'll live so they can rest their horses and clean up themselves. I'll come to help them settle in; Mother has prepared a feast in welcome and we will honor her efforts with hearty appetites!'

"It took but a day or two for Aquila to express approval with his son's choice of friends. He observed them closely as they related to the Arabians without hesitation, patiently gaining their trust while earning the confidence of the men who rode them. In the training corral, Epona worked the colts, guiding them first with the bridle and her voice until she judged them ready for the blanket and saddle.

"In the general order of the day, there was always time for the friends to ride out together discovering the beauty of dazzling vistas and sunlight shimmering on the azure blue of the Aegean. Nuri often begged to accompany them. They all loved the little gypsy and she loved nothing better than a wild gallop across the plain.

"Weeks passed quickly but Azad found himself increasingly restless. He knew he needed to satisfy his wanderlust and seriously test himself as a trader of vision, wit and courage. Epona sensed his agitation and knew that life was about to change. She was content with her horses but at the same time aware of the depth of her feelings for Chenzira. Her life had already evolved beyond her imagination but as a twin, she desired the same extent of satisfaction for her brother.

"They shared the longing of their hearts with each other. Epona gave her blessing to Azad asking only that he help her find the right time and place to reveal her true identity to Chenzira. She needed Azad's presence to affirm the reasoning behind her disguise. Should the truth repel him, she needed Azad's support to help her heal a broken heart.

"It came to pass that the truth was revealed during the foaling of one of the prized mares. Chenzira's own stallion was her sire. Epona had been given the responsibility of assisting at births after demonstrating her skill, sensitivity and good judgment on a number of previous occasions. This birth went on throughout the night. Patience was demanded and gentleness to help the mare pace her labor without fear. Azad kept company with his sister and Chenzira. They talked quietly through the hours creating a calm and confident environment for the animal.

"At last the foal began his sure descent; his mother moaned loudly in her final pushes until he emerged at last. She lay her head down for only a moment's breath before she reached around to begin cleaning her handsome son. Epona stood to stretch, joined by Azad and Chenzira. Deeply moved by the wonder of new life, they found themselves spontaneously coming together in a triumphant embrace.

"Chenzira stood back a moment, gripping Epona by the shoulders and looking levelly first at Azad and then at Epona, he nearly shouted. 'I can't do this anymore! Epona, I know who you are! I've known nearly all this time after catching you once by accident as you bathed alone in a mountain stream. You took my breath away but I understood the wisdom of your disguise so did not seek to betray you on the journey. In all this time you have grown in my respect and admiration as I have come to love you deeply, and so I ask you, Azad, for your sister's hand in marriage.'

"With surprise in his eyes and a chuckle, Azad backed off from the couple, 'Don't ask me! Though we're twins, my sister's life is her own. She's free to choose who she loves.'

"Stunned by the turn of events, Epona moved swiftly back into Chenzira's warm embrace. With his arms around her, she whispered her delight and her love. Behind them the foal was just coming to his legs, his mother nudged his first wobbly attempts. She whinnied her approval, an agreeable witness it seemed, to the full significance of the moment.

"The following day, Chenzira spoke first with his mother. For her beloved first born, she wanted only happiness. Since the day of arrival, she'd been charmed by each of the twins and knew well the high regard in which Aquila held them both. Together, Chenzira and Nofret went to talk with him. He admitted he'd had a hunch but let it be, more concerned with his horses' care and training than in any secret they might harbor. What they held private was their own business, he told his wife and son.

"Such a turn of events was welcome news. It was time for Chenzira to consider marriage but being the headstrong son he was, his parents knew how little influence they could bear in such an important decision. They asked Chenzira to bring Epona to them immediately.

"Quickly, still dressed as a young man because she'd brought no other clothes, Epona approached his parents shyly, holding tightly to Chenzira's arm. Nofret rushed forward to embrace the blushing young woman. Aquila too was beaming his approval. Awkwardly, he hugged her close.

'Well, my dear,' Nofret said smiling, 'the first thing we have to do is dress you in some proper clothes. Nuri!' she called, 'Where are you? Come! You don't want to miss this lovely surprise. We have work to do!'

"Epona remained with Nofret and Nuri the entire day. Nofret insisted on hearing the life story from her future daughter's lips. She was interested in everything - Epona's mother and grandmother, what it was like to grow up as twins, what the land was like and their culture of horses. She listened intently to the way of life engendered by the Great Mother. She likened it to the women's wisdom of her own people and the love they held for their goddess, Isis. She applauded Epona's daring disguise that enabled her to travel safely with Azad on their journey of discovery. Such a longing for freedom would make Epona a good match for Chenzira. In Nofret's own pool, she bathed in rose scented water followed by a massage with precious oils. With impeccable style, Nofret helped her choose the lovely gown she'd wear for Chenzira's first real glimpse of his beloved. Epona reveled in her female body once again.

"Nofret arranged an evening of celebration. Beeswax candles perfumed the air along with abundant sprays of wildflowers; music floated on the breeze - tabla, lyre and flute. Chenzira and Azad entered together not knowing for sure what to expect. Nofret, Aquila and Nuri stood together at the bottom of the stairs that led to their private rooms.

'Where is...' but before he could finish his question, Chenzira's attention was drawn to the stairs and the vision of loveliness that floated towards him. Azad too was stunned, for his sister had changed during the months of their journey. In any case, the clothing of their native land tended more to the practical than the luminous. His sister was not only talented and the companion of his heart, she was beautiful!

"A moment of stilled breath then everyone seemed to talk at once. Laughter filled the hall as Nuri insisted on introducing her new sister!

"The occasion lasted long into the night. Honey and almonds were offered to the goddess to assure fertility and a sweet future. Following the wishes of the couple, they laid the vision for a simple wedding to take place on the cliffs overlooking the Aegean. At Epona's request, Aquila would dispatch a messenger the following morning to Freyda and Canan inviting them to come.

"Amidst the happiness, Aquila expressed concern regarding the response of his soldiers to Epona's transformation. He felt it demanded thoughtful consideration in order to maintain a high level of respect among the ranks. For the majority of Roman men, Epona's position of responsibility, as a woman, would likely be considered immoral.

"Aquila was a man of dignity and honor. He expected the same of his men. To quickly choke out any rumors or ill will, he assured his family he would meet with his officers the following morning then later with the men themselves.

"With such easy camaraderie, Azad felt the time right to share his own plans. He would wait until after the marriage to begin his life as a trader. Aquila expressed regret at losing his talent but assured him that as long as he was Master of Horse, at any garrison anywhere, there would always be opportunity for Azad to return.

"Finally, all said and done, the young people departed. Azad left Chenzira and his sister to walk alone. The evening was sweet; they needed time to digest all that had happened so quickly.

"True to his word, Aquila met with his officers and men. The ability and training skill Epona demonstrated over months had won everyone's respect. Wisely, however, it was decided that she continue to wear men's clothing while at work even as a practical convenience for her. Avoiding any provocation of gender, Epona further suggested that as her hair grew out, she'd wear it wrapped under a cap.

"The weeks passed quickly. A letter was received from Canan with disappointing regrets. At her age, Freyda's bones could no longer tolerate such a journey. Their joy and love were expressed in their gift of a beautiful ruby necklace. The ruby had been a gift from Freyda's father to Behar on the day of their marriage. It had been worn by both Freyda and Canan as brides at their own weddings. The ruby, Canan wrote, is a stone sacred to the Great Mother, a symbol of her life's blood and a blessing of eternal devotion and fruitfulness.

"Nofret and Epona spent many happy hours together planning. Epona was deeply drawn to the culture of Egypt, learning of women's choices and the worship of Isis. Therein she found a comforting parallel to her own native Great Mother. Nofret was delighted with her curiosity and intelligent questions. Sharing Epona's interest with Chenzira, she suggested Egypt for their honeymoon.

"The marriage took place at the spring equinox, lovely in its simplicity. Epona was breath-taking in gossamer silk with a wreath of spring flowers holding her veil. The brilliance of the ruby necklace sparkled like the sun. She rode the Arabian mare whose birthing she had assisted, a gift from Aquila. Chenzira on horseback, led the colt whose birth had enabled this sacred day. Azad accompanied his sister to the altar overlooking the Aegean, presenting the bride to her future husband. Nuri danced before the couple tossing flower petals while Nofret, as priestess of Isis, officiated the ceremony.

"After much feasting and celebration, the couple took a few days to prepare for their journey through Egypt, a gift from Nofret. They crossed the Aegean, first visiting the fabled island of Heraklion before arriving at Alexandria where they stayed a month immersed in the culture of Egypt's shining city of learning and commerce. From Memphis they traveled by luxurious barge down the Nile to their destination, the Isle of Philae and the Temple of Isis.

"With Nofret's advance introduction, they were drawn deeply into the life of the Temple. Priestesses accompanied them to hidden chambers reserved for prayer and ritual. Learning of Epona's interest in midwifery, she was welcomed into the Temple of Hathor where, giving thanks for such synchronicity, she attended at the birth of twins.

She spent several days within the Temple of Mysteries where priestesses were trained according to their aptitude and inclination - music, art, writing, philosophy, healing, prophecy, magic, bee-keeping, midwifery and weather. Awed by the totality of sacred woven through every breath and aspect of life, Epona experienced spiritual surrender.

"After what seemed a lifetime, she rejoined Chenzira. She had so much to share but told him she needed time to absorb all she had learned. Before their departure, they were invited to dine with Layla, High Priestess of the Night. To begin the evening, they were toasted with the finest, golden mead from Temple bees, along with olives, almonds and dates from the island's groves. They learned that Layla and Nofret had been trained together at the Temple from the time they were young girls. While Nofret had chosen the life of marriage with Aquila, Layla had remained. Over the years, Nofret had visited the island on a number of occasions, the last for a dedication ritual to the goddess of her daughter Nuri. Until death, Layla and Nofret would remain sisters of Isis in spirit.

"Chenzira expressed surprise at all that Layla shared about his mother. Layla urged him to consider the equality of women and their right to choose the life to which they are most inspired. 'For true contentment in marriage,' she told him, 'men and women need be equal partners, respectful of each other's gifts. Devotion, awareness, kindness, fairness - these are just some of the attributes of a successfully balanced endeavor whether it be religious, political or the contract of marriage.

'Think upon these concepts now, especially since you have just joined your life together with this beautiful and gifted young woman. Though called by different names, Epona honors the Great Mother as deeply as Nofret and I honor Isis. In all of nature there is no life without the union of male and female. It is true in heaven and it is true on earth.'

"Chenzira was silent through all she spoke. Deeply moved, he looked to Epona as if seeing her for the first time. He had a momentary glimpse of his parents and understood in that brief vision, the truth of what Layla had spoken. Taking Epona's hand, he bowed his head, then looking directly at her asked for Layla's blessing upon their marriage.

"Now, my sweet daughter and granddaughter, I see you are both tired. There is more story yet to tell but let's all lie down now and get some rest."

"Nana, you have told us so much! I feel as if I know every one of them!" Mary said with an animated yawn.

"There is power when women dream together, Mary." Sakinah told her. "Perhaps you'll have a visitor tonight, maybe from the little gypsy or even Epona herself. Though they lived generations ago, they are each a part of your family. May the angels watch over us all this night; sleep in peace, dear ones."

The following morning dawned dark and gloomy. Clouds hung heavy, warning of an impending storm. Early risers sensed the deluge to come and decided that the weather itself suggested a day of rest. There were sufficient tents to house the women and children and the men quickly raised a lean-to, to protect the fire, keeping it banked underneath so it could be brought back to power as soon as the storm passed.

Joseph came with Mary to Sakinah's tent. "I'd like Mary to spend the time with you if that's alright. One of the supply wagons needs repair especially if tomorrow the going will be through mud. I have work to do and I know she'd like your company."

Mary sprung up from where she lay. "Of course! Nana is telling stories and Mary will be able to rest and hear them with us."

Hannah joined in, "Come warm up when you finish your work, Joseph. You know Mary's welcome! We'll make sure she's comfortable and gets the most out of this day of rest. It will be good for her. I've already brewed tea. Would you like some Joseph, before you go out in the storm?"

"Thank you, Hannah, Mary already provided tea and breakfast. Let me leave you with some extra blankets and the folding backrest I made for her."

Mary helped her mother arrange a warm little nest of a bed then helped Mary settle in. The backrest, lightweight and clever, assured her comfort. The day promised to be a long one.

"So, Mary, now that we have you all to ourselves, how are you doing?" Sakinah asked.

"Oh... this weather has me in the grip of melancholy, I'm afraid."

Looking at her closely, and taking her hand gently, Sakinah ventured further, "How so?"

Mary's eyes grew big, her chin began to tremble and before they knew it, the tears were coming in a deluge to mirror the weather outside. Sakinah wrapped her arms around her until the sobbing subsided and she could speak. "My ankles are swollen, my back hurts all the time, my breasts ache and, and... and... I miss my mother!" The tears began streaming again.

The child Mary stood at her feet astonished, watching while Sakinah and her mother let Mary cry her eyes out. At last she began to quiet. With a little smile, Hannah offered a cup of tea and wrapped another blanket around her shoulders to ease the shudders.

"Take a sip of this, it will ease your fears and loneliness. We can help you with some of what you're experiencing. You're near to birthing your babe, what you're feeling is natural and experienced by all pregnant women."

Hannah adjusted the backrest and suggested, "Here, Mary lie back against the rest, close your eyes and let your breathing deepen." Mary did as she was told.

In a soothing whisper Hannah leaned in, "That's it... that's right, Mary... just keep breathing... ahhh... that's good. Better now?" Mary nodded her head, looked up and smiled shyly, appearing more like the child she was than the mother she was soon to be.

"So you miss your mother, Mary." Sakinah asked directly. "Why wasn't she able to come with us to Bethlehem?"

"Her cousin Elizabeth gave birth a few months ago." Mary answered. "Elizabeth is old, and my mother, Anna is her only woman relation still alive. Mother knew I'd be in good hands with the two of you traveling with me so she made the hard choice. I understand why she's not here but I miss her so much!" Tears clearly threatened to spill again but the intensity of her emotional storm was over. She settled back sighing deeply as she closed her eyes. Her face slowly let go its tension and she relaxed.

As Hannah moved about the tent brewing a pot of chamomile tea and preparing a poultice of birth root to ease the tenderness in her breasts, Sakinah quietly assured her, "Mary, there are things we can do to ease some of your discomfort. All women suffer to a certain extent with the aches you describe. We brought a variety of herbs and ointments that we'll massage into your feet and your back. Your breasts hurt because they're full and ready to nourish your infant. Up until now, you've been focused on your baby and the future altogether as a family with Joseph of concern to you as well. This trip was a stress you didn't need but had to accommodate. You've reached the point where your own emotions are so powerful you can't deny them any longer. Your breath, Mary, is really the key to keeping you comfortable. Anxiety will diminish as you absorb the life force energy of the breath. Hannah and I are here to help you from right now all the way through the birth."

Mary opened her eyes to accept the tea, watching while Sakinah poured a generous amount of almond oil into a bowl then added a few drops of lavender and rose oil. The fragrance flowed gently through the tent, relaxing any remaining tension. "Child, come here to me. Now we need your help."

Mary, who'd been standing stock still watching, responded in a flash, relieved to be drawn at last into the intimacy of the moment. "Watch as I pour this scented oil into the palm of my hands and rub them together." Uncovering Mary's bare feet, she took one in her hands and began massaging gently. "See how I work my fingers and thumbs together, surrounding each toe and how I get deeply into the sole with pressure from my thumb. Your hands are small but strong. Use your strength to rub circles slowly and in deep. Pay attention to what your hands are doing but watch Mary's face from time to time to make sure your efforts create pleasure not pain."

Mary watched her grandmother closely, observing the calm manipulations until Sakinah indicated that she could take over the other foot. Sakinah watched her granddaughter begin with more confidence than reservation. Approving her motions, she moved from the foot of the bed to sit beside Mary and Hannah.

"Tell us about your mother, Mary." Sakinah encouraged, "your sharing may help create a sense of her presence."

Mary, restored to calm and enjoying the lovely indulgence of the child's massage began to speak, "My mother Anna, is a wise woman, the heart of our home and equal partner to her husband Joachim, my father. In our family, mother and father listen to each other's hearts before deciding important matters together. On this journey, as Mary rides with me, she's sharing your stories. From the time of my first flow and through all the moon times since, I've learned of *Shekinah,* the female soul of God. Mother tells me that even among our own people there are those who disregard and even deny the sacred feminine experiencing the loss of balance, talent, justice and harmony not only in family life but in the larger circle of community. In our home, ancient wisdom prevails. Father loves, honors and respects the mystery of woman, understanding how it is only through the blessed union of male and female that life is created holy.

"My betrothal to Joseph a year ago was a blessing. From the Temple, my father knew Joseph's father Jacob and my mother shared moon times with his mother. Anna recognized the kinship of balance, love and respect that existed in their marriage as in her own. It was our mothers together who suggested the match to our fathers. Though he's older, I'm comfortable with Joseph's maturity and inspired by his talent as a carpenter. Joseph and I found each other pleasing and so the contract was agreed upon by us together.

When the angel came to tell me I had found favor with God and was to bear a son named Jesus, I was troubled because I was yet an unmarried virgin. He assured me that the Holy Spirit would come upon me. Trusting in God, I humbly accepted the angel's word and he departed.

Awakening from the experience in near terror, I ran to my mother and shared the news. She was not surprised as it had been foretold to her in dreams. Holding me close, she assured me of the holiness of my acceptance. She promised she would consult with Joseph's mother in the morning. That night, the angel visited with Joseph also in a dream, sharing his awesome message of the birth of Jesus while reassuring him of my purity.

With our families together, we decided to marry right away. During the few days of preparation, my mother was with me constantly easing my fears. She shared the ancient prophecy that foretold the birth of a king, to a virgin of the House of David, a king who would rule over Jacob's descendants, a rule that would never end. Though I had accepted the angel's word (*what else could I do!*) it was my mother's strength and confidence that carried me through the wedding and especially the first months of pregnancy. It was Anna who knew of Hannah's skills as a nearby midwife. Through Hannah, you have come into my life, Sakinah, along with the blessed child Mary who keeps me grounded with her innocence and joy."

At the mention of her name, Mary looked up from her task. Gently she pulled the covers back over Mary's feet. Hannah leaned forward bringing her daughter to her feet and, returning to sit beside Sakinah, she drew the child into her lap.

"Life is a mystery, Mary." Sakinah said. "Though our origins and culture vary, we each have traveled many roads to come together at this auspicious time. We too know well the ancient prophecy. In common, through our life choices, we honor the creative force of the Queen of Heaven, the Great Mother, Isis, Shekinah; by whatever name we use, She is present always as is our Lord. They live in us and we in them. It is through their sacred union, that we are blessed for all eternity."

At this point, Joseph stuck his head in the tent. "How are things in here?" he asked. "It seems the rain is coming to an end. I'm still needed with the other men."

Sakinah went to the entrance of the tent assuring him that all was well. "Mary is nearly asleep, Joseph. Let her rest here comfortably with us. This day has been good for her. We'll return her to you in good spirits when you're finished with your tasks."

Turning back to Mary, Sakinah suggested sleep. "Hannah has prepared these poultices to ease the ache in your breasts. Their warmth will comfort you and with the rest of this almond, lavender and rose oil, I'll rub your back a bit. The sleep that comes will refresh you in every way giving you renewed strength as we resume our journey tomorrow."

Mary, noticing the child asleep on her mother's lap, nodded to both women. Understanding, Hannah lifted her daughter onto the bed. Mary rolled to her side nestling the child into the curve of her body while opening her robe so that Sakinah could massage her back with the oils. Her eyes closed and in moments the sound of their joined breath was rhythmic and peaceful.

The rain stopped by late afternoon and soon the warmth of the sun called everyone out from damp quarters. It was little Mary who first spied the rainbow arcing across the sky. Her ecstatic exclamations echoed through the camp drawing everyone's attention to the sky. Nature's glorious spectrum in all its wonder was perceived as a welcome gift and promise. Spirits were high that evening as clothes were hung to dry, the fire built back up and the aroma of food began to wind its way through the camp.

After the evening meal, a doumbek (drum) and few tambourines were set up to warm by the fire; the players began with a slow and beckoning rhythm. Before long they were accompanied by the sounds of sistrum (rattle), flute and lyre. Men and women clapped the cadence and bodies soon began to stand and sway. Hannah grabbed her daughter, drawing her to her feet. Eyes alight, they joined the dance as it wove gracefully around the central fire.

Joseph and Mary walked over to join Sakinah as she watched the dancers, beaming a smile of pleasure. Seeing them all together, Hannah and Mary left the circle to join them. With a light of playfulness in her eyes, Hannah drew them into a circle of their own with Joseph's Mary in the center. Holding hands they moved in step surrounding her in love, swaying in response to the ancient heart beat pulse of life and the son she soon would birth.

The travelers were up and on their way with the first light of dawn. This day's walk would mark the halfway point on their journey; they eagerly anticipated their destination. They traveled easily, enjoying the gentle breeze, grateful for the hint of warmth. Mary again insisted on walking. Holding hands with little Mary, they made use of the walking stick for balance over uneven ground. Occasionally, the child would leave her side to pick wildflowers which she wove into a circlet for Mary to wear.

At an afternoon rest stop the two Marys knelt together on the ground appearing to share secrets like sisters. Hannah observed their curious activity and watched as Mary jumped up excited, dusted herself off and then helped the pregnant Mary to her feet with the aid of the staff between them for support. Intrigued, she looked forward to hearing about it after supper.

Finally, the day's work accomplished, Sakinah, Hannah and Mary were gathered again at the fire. Mary spoke up first, impatient to share her news. "Nana, I want to hear more about Epona and Chenzira but I'm so excited! Mary's been listening to my stories and today she showed me a symbol that represents the wholeness of father and mother in union just like you're telling me in our stories. Let me show you!"

Taking hold of a nearby twig, she carefully drew a downward triangle - △ "This represents the grace of God, our Great Father, descending upon us like rain to nurture seeds of love."

Then she drew an upward triangle -▽ "This represents Shekinah, the Great Mother. Her body is open, like a chalice, ready to receive God's grace, the gift of life.

"Now watch! I put one on top of the other and look what happens... ✡... a hexagon in perfect balance! In its center is where the seed of life takes root, protected and holy. Mary calls it '*the as above, so below*'. The hexagon is magic. It's just like the honeycomb that makes a perfect nest for the Queen and all the eggs she lays that will become bees that will make more honey! So it's even like the circle too that has no beginning and no end. It's what I want next on my staff. Can we do it now before you begin with Epona?"

Touched by Mary's articulate interpretation, Sakinah proceeded to help her burn the image onto the staff. With Hannah, they admired the handiwork and its depth of meaning. "Thank you, Nana, it's beautiful."

Settling down, Hannah and Mary got comfortable before Sakinah began. "So, my dear one, where were we?"

"Layla had just given her blessing to the marriage. I think it's probably time they began their journey home."

"And so it was. With so many experiences to assimilate, the couple turned their hearts to home, eager to share highlights with family. They'd been gone for months and would likely not set foot back in Thessaloniki for another month. They luxuriated in the slow passage up the Nile but crossing the Aegean was arduous. The water was rough; Epona was seasick most of the trip. Chenzira did his best to make her comfortable but all she longed for was solid ground. Chenzira was able to get a message to Aquila of their expected arrival.

"The winds were kind during the final two days of the trip so when at last they docked at their destination, Epona was presentable. Except for Azad, away on a trade route, the entire family was there when the ship sailed into port. In spite of her high spirits, Nofret could not help but notice Epona's weight loss and fatigue. Nevertheless she welcomed her with open arms leaving such concern for a later conversation. Nuri was beside herself with excitement and rushed into her brother's arms at first sight, thrilled to have them both back.

"Aquila had wisely arranged for a night's lodging before the final return to the garrison. Love, nourishment and a good night's sleep readied everyone for the trip home. Nofret, Nuri and Epona rode together in a spacious passenger chariot, enabling them to keep to a faster pace with Aquila and Chenzira on horseback. Lo and behold, when they drove through the gates, there was Azad waiting for them. Surviving the longest separation of their lives, Azad knew he *must* be there to welcome his sister home.

"Within a few days' time, life settled back into its glorious routine. Epona returned to her beloved horses, an ambitious training schedule and the pleasure of afternoon rides into the countryside with Chenzira, Azad and Nuri. Observing closely, Nofret was quick to take note of her continuing bouts of nausea which Epona brushed off as simply *getting her legs back* after such a rough passage. It was only a week before Nofret took Epona aside for a mother/daughter conversation. She wasted no time. 'My dear, have you given any thought to the possibility that you're pregnant?'

"Epona, stopped in her tracks, stared with wide eyes. 'Pregnant? Could that explain why I'm sick and so tired in the afternoons? Oh, my! Pregnant? Can it be? Really? Nofret! I'm pregnant! I am! How could I not know? I'm a midwife for heaven's sake! I'm going to have a baby … Chenzira's baby … our baby! Oh, thank you, Nofret!'

'Don't thank me, sweetheart!' Laughing heartily Nofret continued, 'I think you better go share the news with your husband. It seems his eyes are as blind as yours have been. Before you go, a blessing! You are my dear daughter and now you will make me a grandmother. Such a gift you have brought back with you! May Isis, the Great Mother bless and keep you safe. Go with speed now to tell Chenzira!'

"Over the next weeks, reality settled in. The bouts of morning sickness diminished and Epona's energy surged. She continued working with the horses but allowed herself time to rest each afternoon. Often she spent the time visiting with Nofret, questioning her about Layla, their enduring friendship, the training they'd received as priestesses of Isis and the individual choices they'd made.

Dedicated to the goddess at birth and as the daughter of a priestess, Epona learned that Nuri too would be initiated in Philae. Nofret would take her there when she turned seven. After seven more years of training at fourteen, Nuri could choose for herself the life she wanted to live. 'Suppose I birth a girl child ..." Epona mused, "to love and raise her for seven years then allow her to learn among the women a way of life with value, honor, purpose and sacred all woven together.'

She and Chenzira discussed the possibility. Raised by Nofret and having himself visited the sanctuary, he was comfortable with the idea. 'But perhaps, my sweet, we will have a son!'

'How do men learn of the mystery of life and all that's holy?' she bantered.

'Why, from our mothers, of course, if we're lucky enough to be born to one as wise as Nofret. Aquila, though he respected his mother, grew up in the Roman culture and had much to learn when they first married. She's told us often, laughing at how much work he was in the early days. He had to learn how to release unreasonable expectations and to understand the value of the true partnership she offered to the marriage. Look at them now! You and I, we have a good foundation and a long future before us. I will cherish you always and respect your choices especially in regards to our daughter, though it's likely we'll have a son, you just wait and see.'

"And so it came to pass that Epona birthed a son. Strong, vigorous and healthy, they named him Valens. His hair was black like his father, Nuri and Aquila. His eyes were blue like his mother and the Aegean. He was fearless, first carried in a sling next to his mother's heart while she returned to training the horses; soon, like his mother, he was pulling himself to standing holding onto their tails. Seated in front of his father, he loved the rhythm of the horse, first at a canter then squealing delight as they broke into a gallop. Nuri, already six, had her own horse and joined them often on their wild rides by the edge of the sea.

"When the time came for Nofret to take Nuri to the Isle of Philae, Valens was three and Epona was pregnant again. This time she was sure it would be a girl. Her pregnancy was difficult. Morning sickness lingered. She lost weight and her increasing fatigue prohibited her working with the horses she loved. With Nofret gone to Egypt, she became despondent. Chenzira and Valens did their best to keep her spirits up but she wanted Nofret's company; she wanted her mother!

"The time of birthing arrived and it was indeed a girl. A trusted midwife attended the birth but Epona cried for Nofret. Though an urgent message had been sent to Philae, she had not been able to return in time. The labor was long and hard. Epona suffered a great loss of blood. The child was born with a caul, a momentous and rare occasion signifying that the child would likely have supersensory abilities and the gift of prophecy. The midwife had never experienced such a birth but she knew to save the veil as a powerful talisman.

Epona's daughter was as strong and healthy as her mother was weak. The midwife ministered to her with growing concern unable to staunch the flow of blood that continued even after delivery of the placenta. Chenzira was called to her bedside.

"Epona smiled weakly as Chenzira held his baby daughter for the first time. She had hair the color of honey like all her mothers before her. They named her Mellitza, meaning sweetness.

'You must remember our agreement, Chenzira. Nofret will be so sad she wasn't here. Be gentle with her and don't let her get lost in guilt or grief. Mellitza will need her to be both mother and grandmother. Nofret will know when the time is right to bring her to the Temple. You have been the best of husbands, Chenzira. I am so sad to leave you and Valens, Azad and your father. Come lie here and hold me. I will nurse our beautiful Mellitza this once so she will never forget the feel and taste and smell of the mother who loves her.'

"With that Epona took the baby to her breast and laying back on the pillow with Chenzira's arms around her, she closed her eyes, her face relaxed and she breathed no more."

"NO!" Mary sat up straight, tears glistened and began to fall. "No, Nana! What happened? Why? Epona … no … Oh! I am so sad!" Hannah held her until she quieted.

"It happens sometimes, Mary. Birth and death are mystical journeys. If we allow ourselves to surrender to the divine we can come to understand the choices our souls make. This kind of outcome can happen even with a skilled and loving midwife in attendance.

"Let me share words of ancient wisdom to provide insight and comfort, *'For everything there is a season and a time for every matter under heaven: a time to be born, and a time to die; a time to plant, and a time to pluck up what is planted; a time to weep, and a time to laugh; a time to mourn and a time to dance.'* (Ecclesiastes 3: 1-2, 4)

"Mary, over time you'll learn to sway and dance with the ebb and flow of life's seasons. For this moment in Epona's story, trust that the purpose of her earth journey is accomplished and that her child Mellitza will be loved. Her family will grieve the loss of such a loving spirit as Epona but turn your focus now to Mellitza, a child who will thrive in the life that surrounds her. Nofret will return, and with the wisdom of the Mother Father God, will restore a world in balance with love as the foundation."

"Nana, does this mean that Mary's baby can die before he even lives?"

"The birth of Mary's baby has been foretold in prophecy for generations upon generations. He comes to create a new way of living. We will be there to help Mary through her labor and to bring this babe safely into the loving arms of family.

In coming to know Mary, you have been touched by her spirit, humility, courage and willingness. Only time will tell how such prophecy will impact our lives. For now we have all been blessed to travel this road together. The love that's developed between you and Mary is an unexpected gift. Be fearless! Let yourself be open to go wherever your path may lead. Remember the intention for your staff as well as the stories of the mothers who have gone before you. Therein you will find comfort, strength and understanding."

Exhausted by the sadness of Epona's sudden death, Mary sought only to be cradled by her mother until she was asleep. Hannah carried her into the tent and placed her lovingly within the warmth of her sleeping roll where she slumbered deeply until daybreak. Throughout the following day, Mary was reserved and stayed close to her mother and Sakinah.

Mary finally broke her silence after the evening meal. "Nana, tell me about choices. Did Epona really choose to die?"

"Just as the union of our Great Mother and Father is eternal," Sakinah began, "we believe that our souls are immortal. Thus they never die. Each of us has a purpose for our life on earth and freedom to choose. In order to manifest such purpose, we make important choices before we even come into our bodies, choosing family as well as the time and place of our birth.

"We come through the gateway of birth as forgetful babes needing to grow and learn even as we slowly come to remember. The loving family surrounds and supports us in that process so that gradually we come not only to remember but to develop and experience the character, values and lessons needed to accomplish our soul's purpose on earth.

"Elder souls may choose a path of tremendous challenge demanding courage, strength, compassion and generosity. No matter the choice, in every life there will be times of loss and sadness, just like you learned yesterday.

"How we move through such times is also a choice. In the case of Epona, the family will mourn of course, but because Mellitza's very life is at stake, they will choose the path of joy, beauty, strength and loving kindness so that Mellitza will grow with a foundation of wholeness and harmony.

"So, to answer your question, 'did Epona really *choose* to die?' let me say that we who are left behind can often find it difficult to accept that one so happy and loving *would choose to die* rather than to live because we miss them so much. But understand that the grief we feel is our own. The soul is free, released back to our Great Mother Father God.

"It is not for us to understand the soul contracts that others make on behalf of their life purpose. Sometimes life itself is the most generous gift one can give on behalf of another to help them further their own.

"All this can feel confusing Mary. You're young to be contemplating such matters. You'll grow in wisdom as you grow in body. Listen to your inner voice in all matters and trust the answers you receive before blindly following tradition simply for tradition's sake. The prophecy of Jesus' coming promises to usher in a new way. *'Then when you call upon me and come and pray to me, I will hear you. When you search for me, you will find me; if you seek me with all your heart.'* (Jeremiah 29: 12, 13). Therein lies the *nous.* Look beneath the surface and the truth shall be revealed."

Mary sat attentively throughout Sakinah's lengthy explanation. Thoughtfully she whispered, "So, Nana, do you think I am an 'Elder Soul'? I don't remember doing it but if what you say is true, my choosing Hannah and Ari as parents and you as my grandmother makes me truly blessed. Yes?"

Hannah, who'd been listening closely hugged her daughter to her heart. With a twinkle in her eye and a nod of agreement she looked to her own mother gratefully acknowledging the wisdom of her teachings.

Revived of spirit, Mary stood up with resolve to bring her staff to the firelight. "There's something else to be added to my staff, Nana. I want to burn a dot in the center of the *as above/so below.* The dot will remind me of both Mellitza and Baby Jesus, safe within the loving arms of the Great Mother Father God wherein they will discover their true purpose."

"Nofret arrived home the following day; too late, too late. She held her son and grandson as they grieved hard in her embrace. Aquila was at hand throughout the ordeal providing his strength to the mix of tears and heartache.

"Chenzira had already attended to a wet nurse for the baby. The midwife, still with the family, spent time with Nofret to share the experience, answering all the questions. She brought forth the mysterious veil that had covered Mellitza's face at the birth but could find no connection between such a rarity and Epona's death. Satisfied that the midwife had acted wisely with all the skill she herself might have brought to bear had she been there, Nofret sent her home.

"She then engaged Chenzira's loving touch in the rituals that would release Epona's soul from her body - cleansing, anointing, embalming and wrapping her for burial. Nuri was informed by Layla but since she'd just arrived, it was agreed that she stay at Philae and pray for Epona from the sanctuary of the Temple.

"Azad had returned as soon as he'd received the news. He was beside himself with grief. Chenzira spent time with him listening as Azad poured forth his undying love and gratitude for his twin. Nofret's suggestion that he take Mellitza to meet her grandmother at some future time seemed to lift him from his darkness.

"Nofret told him she'd journey with him. Chenzira immediately spoke up that he would join them bringing Valens too so both children could learn of the loving foundation that had so influenced their mother's life.

"During the time it took to create a fitting sarcophagus, letters were written by each of the family to place within the coffin. A lock of hair from each of her children was put inside her final wrappings along with a hank of horsetail from her beautiful mare. Chenzira and Azad each provided a talisman of personal remembrance. Azad sprinkled a pouch of earth he'd brought from their homeland having kept it close to his heart for so many years. It was decided that the ruby necklace, worn at her wedding, would be saved as a future gift for Mellitza.

'Mellitza was nearly three months old when they laid her mother to rest. Already a knowing light sparkled from her blue eyes. She gazed at each of her family with compassion, lessening their pain with the sweetness of her smile.

"When Mellitza was a sturdy, mischievous toddler, Nofret decided it was time for the journey to meet Canan, her grandmother. Already she was exhibiting her mother's fearlessness and way with horses; especially Epona's mare. They seemed to know each other. The horse would come to nuzzle her whenever she approached. Mellitza loved Valens, her protective big brother but worried him ceaselessly with her daring. She liked nothing better than galloping full speed ahead, albeit riding safely up front, secure in his saddle. She could sense anyone's mood at a given moment and already recognized she had the power to affect change with just the twinkle of an eye. She could speak Greek by the time she was a year old and at two, was conversing fluently in Greek, Nofret's Coptic and even some of her uncle's native tongue. It was time to go home.

"Azad led the way as the family set out on horseback. In spite of the reason for their travels, there was a festive air and high spirits to support them on their journey of return. The weather was pleasing and the horses eager. To pass the time, Azad and Chenzira challenged each other to feats of speed and prowess. Six year old Valens was not to be ignored and demanded that he too be allowed to test his skills.

"Their party, with crew to handle tents, cooks for meals and a number of soldiers for protection, was large enough that they were nearly a caravan unto themselves but often at the end of a day, they sometimes preferred to join up with another group already comfortably encamped along the route. The night times were exciting when instruments came out enticing jugglers and acrobats to entertain. Nofret with sistrum, timbrel (tambourine) and lyre never hesitated to enter the cultural milieu while Mellitza, drawn by the irresistible rhythms was usually the first to dance. She loved being the center of attention!

"Traveling together for the first time, they had decided to make the trip a memorable adventure for each of them. Azad, knowing the route well, would often take them off the beaten path to discover villages, landmarks, waterfalls, mountain peaks and hidden valleys of exquisite beauty. They bathed in mountain streams and sometimes slept under the stars. They met with artisans and weavers who Azad had come to know on previous trips. Nofret added to her cache of gifts she was bringing to Canan and home for Nuri to be sent onto Philae. Over the weeks on the road Azad shared many exotic tales of his homeland. He missed Epona deeply as only a twin can; they had shared everything including their mother's womb. He looked forward to being with his mother again; they would hold each other's sorrow even as they delighted in Valens and Mellitza.

"As they neared their destination, a courier was sent ahead to inform the village of their approaching arrival. One more night under the stars gave opportunity for Nofret to bathe the children and to gather the gifts she was bringing. Around the fire that night, Azad shared stories of their mother's childhood, the wild adventures and the tricks they'd played on each other. While Valens had some memories of his own, Mellitza knew her mother only through the family's stories. She was astounded to hear that her mother had cut off her beautiful hair to travel safely as Azad's twin brother. How brave! How clever!

"The following morning just as they broke camp and mounted their horses for the final ride in to the village, the sound of pounding hoof beats could be heard riding hard in their direction. The soldiers immediately came to attention, ready to protect the family from danger.

"Azad, with a sixth sense, leaped ahead grinning ear to ear. There was Canan, riding to welcome them, tall in the saddle, ageless. Horse and rider were breath-taking! Near enough, Azad and Canan jumped from their mounts into a wild embrace, tears flowing amidst smiles, laughter and cries of excitement. Together!

"Nofret and Chenzira held back allowing mother and son their first emotional moments of bittersweet reunion. Before the children could get restless, Azad brought his mother to meet her grandchildren and introduce the people he loved. After a few moments of shyness, mutual appraisal and talking at once, everyone mounted up again for the final few miles to home.

"In the time Azad had been away, provoked by visits from so many travelers coming through the village, Canan had learned to speak a halting Greek of benefit especially since she was now chief among the elders. Communication would be easier than expected.

"When they arrived back at the village, Canan came first to Nofret. They stood face to face looking deeply into each other's eyes as if taking stock. The strength, power and integrity they saw in each other promised a lifetime of friendship. Canan turned then to Chenzira, the man her daughter had loved. Knowing her daughter, she recognized the character of honesty, tenderness, intelligence and wholeness he must be made of to be loved at all by Epona. Seeing that strength in his eyes and stature, she welcomed her son.

"After the initial introductions, Canan took her grandchildren by the hand and walked with them through the town proudly introducing them to everyone they met on the way.

"The village itself was rustic. Descended from nomads, they had only in the last few generations begun putting down roots. Structures were comfortable and solid, made of stone with two or three rooms, windows for light, fireplaces for heat and cooking and thatched roofs over all. Fenced gardens were organized and thriving, tended carefully by the women. There was a flowing river nearby for fresh water and bathing. By afternoon, Nofret and the children were settled comfortably in a cabin. After all the excitement of the day, it was easy to put them down for a refreshing nap.

"Nofret emerged, curious to discover more about Epona's people. Azad and Chenzira were off tending to the horses. Nofret walked slowly through the village acknowledging the stares with smiles and nods. Occasionally a few words were exchanged. Tall, Egyptian and elegant, she was definitely a foreigner but everyone knew who she was, how she had welcomed Epona and Azad and that Valens and Mellitza were grandchildren both to her and to Canan, their Chief Elder. Though the folk were reserved, she and Chenzira were welcome and would come to be known by everyone.

"Canan joined her shortly. 'There is someone you must meet now, Nofret.' Taking her by the hand, Canan guided her down a forest path that led close to the river.

Honeybees drew nectar from the wild flowers that edged the water and dragonflys with glittering wings hung low in the air, afraid of nothing as the women passed by. Shortly they came upon a structure built of stone, set back in a grove with a view of the water. A wizened old woman was sitting outside smoking a pipe. 'This is my mother, Freyda. It surprises us all that she's still with us, perhaps she's been waiting for the return of the twins. She knows of Epona's death but has not yet reunited with Azad. In fact, he doesn't even know she's still alive. He'll meet with her later.

'Mother, I want you to meet Nofret. She is also grandmother to Epona's children, Valens and Mellitza. She and Epona's beloved Chenzira have traveled all this way with Azad and the children to meet us.'

"Freyda turned slowly to scrutinize the visitor. Like her daughter, she looked beneath the surface. Nofret, astonished by the depth of her gaze and the clarity of her blue eyes, was rewarded with a near toothless grin and an ancient blue-veined hand extended in welcome. Nofret went forward on her knees, taking the offered hand to her heart and bowing her head in a gesture of respect.

"With Canan translating, Freyda spoke, 'You loved my granddaughter Epona, like a mother. I can see your heart is pure. Together, we mourn the loss of our bright spirit yet we know her soul lives on, safe within the heart of the Great Mother. You are brave and kind and gladden our hearts more than you know by traveling such a distance so we may know of her life, her children and the man Chenzira, your son, who was her love. You are welcome here until all questions are answered. Know that forever because of such love, we are joined together as family.'

'Over the years, Epona and I had many conversations about your Great Mother.' Nofret began slowly. 'I am a priestess of Isis, who is *our* Great Mother in all of Egypt. Your daughter and I, along with my youngest Nuri, related on every level because we hold the Mother's energy as sacred. It is the foundation of our home and although my husband Aquila is a Roman, he and our son Chenzira have lived their lives honoring the power, balance, goodness and grace of the Great Goddess Mother. Nuri, in fact, has just begun her initiations at the Temple of Isis on the Isle of Philae.

'I was just returning from Egypt when I received word of Epona's difficult birth but to my great sadness, I was not able to get back in time. I must share with you that Mellitza was born with a caul. As a talisman of power, it has been safely preserved. In fact, I brought it along thinking you would want to feel the energy yourselves to gain insight into your granddaughter. Among our people such a birth foretells the gift of prophecy, an ability to see beyond the veil, a heightened sensitivity to the voice of spirit, and the power to bring healing to the sick. With such aptitudes comes great responsibility. Training is essential to maintain purity of spirit. Though such a birth is rare, I wonder what experience either of you may have with such an occurrence.'

"Freyda sat forward with great attention. 'You might have heard the story of how I came as a small child from the far north with my father, Norman, a merchant and widower. His heart was heavy with the loss of his beloved, my birth mother. We wandered for some time before we were mystically drawn to this village, called by Behar, the Seer of our people. She too had been born with the caul. Her mother and grandmother knew well the portent of such a birth and guided her even as a young child, to listen without fear to her inner knowing and to trust the voices that spoke to her. All her life she used her gifts to the benefit of our people as a healer, a midwife and our ritual leader.

'She was a relatively young woman and beautiful when she began dreaming of my father and of me, the child she longed to raise for she already knew she was barren. While she gave freely to those she assisted, her heart longed for the intimacy of her own family. Our arrival was the answer to *all* of our prayers. Behar and my father were joined in a joyous ceremony, twin hearts who discovered each other through trusting the power of spirit and the wisdom of the Great Mother. I was embraced as the miracle of her life. I loved her dearly in return.

'I would very much like to hold the veil that covered the face of my great-granddaughter at birth but first I want to meet her and her father, who Epona chose to be her husband. I understand there is also a grandson. I look forward to holding them all close to this old heart of mine. Blessed Be! In truth, I am blessed to have more to love even at the age I am!'

"Placing her hands tenderly on her mother's shoulders, Canan smiled. 'Azad is here as well, Mother. He has yet to learn that you are still alive! You must keep your heart open wide to embrace all that the Great Mother is bringing home to you at this time. Let's not forget the matriarch of this family too. Nofret, with the love and insight of your Isis, you bring much healing to us all. Tonight you will be guests at a feast with fire, food, games, music and dancing to celebrate the goodness of our lives!'

"With that, they left Freyda to her thoughts and the lovely afternoon allowing her to rest before the festivities ahead.

"During the weeks of their visit, Nofret and Canan bared their souls, each learning from the other. Their talks often took place by the river so Freyda could be with them. The children were crazy for the horses and exulted in the attention and time both Azad and Chenzira had to teach them tricks on horseback. Sometimes they'd join the women by the river and soon both Valens and Mellitza were strong swimmers. One lazy afternoon as Mellitza slept soundly on a blanket by her grandmothers' feet, a honeybee buzzed her head seeking a taste of her sweetness. In brushing it off, she was *kissed* on the lips.

"While Canan soothed the child and calmly removed the stinger, Freyda reached down for a few plantain leaves, a common weed that grew profusely at the river's edge. She put them in her mouth, chewed momentarily then placed the masticated leaves over the wound. Nofret snuggled her close as they all distracted her with silly antics and rhymes. Before long, she was up joining the fun, her pain forgotten.

"Once the crisis was over the women smiled among themselves. It was the stuff of bee lore that a child stung on the lips would grow to have the power of persuasive speech, capable of great influence due to the sweetness of her words.

"With deep appreciation for each other's way of life, the time for return was soon upon them. Their expanded family was Epona's gift. On the new moon after the harvest, Nofret and Canan together led a ritual and spiral dance with all the village. The horses were blessed for a safe journey home. The ceremony gave thanks for the bounty of their fields, their bonding as a family, Epona's memory and the gift of her children whose lives would honor her memory and the wisdom of the Great Mother.

"The morning they left, the children were each riding horses gifted by their grandmother Canan; Mellitza on a dappled mare and Valens on a roan stallion. At Azad's suggestion, the Arabians on which they'd arrived were given to Canan to strengthen the native herd. All the village turned out for their departure even Freyda who arrived for the farewell blessing.

"After all they had experienced, the adults rode out silently, wrapped in cloaks of reflection. Recognizing each other's need for private reverie, they allowed the children freedom to ride ahead learning the personalities of their new horses. Small by comparison to the Arabians, they were slower but strong, sturdy and responsive; especially well-suited for bodies their size. The level of their excitement lifted everyone's spirits so that by the second morning everyone was up and eager, their sights finally turned towards home.

"The trip seemed longer on the return so ready were they for the familiar sights and sounds of their beloved Thessaloniki and of course Aquila! They were looking forward to sharing the highlights of their journey. As they neared their destination, a soldier was dispatched to the garrison provoking Aquila to ride out himself, so eager was he to reunite with Nofret and his family. Together, they spent the last night under the stars. With great jubilation the following morning, they reentered the garrison gates.

"Life returned quickly to its balance and routine but it was only a matter of time before Azad was ready to get back on the road. His wagons were loaded to bursting with treasures. Nofret suggested the possibility of a bonding love but he laughed, insisting that his wanderlust would make that unlikely unless he could meet a woman of equal curiosity and the blood of a nomad flowing through her veins. With Azad's departure, Nofret turned her full attention to the children. Chenzira was always an attentive and loving father.

"The years passed. When Mellitza was five, Nofret began to talk with Chenzira about her training in Egypt. She knew it would be difficult for him to let her go but he would be true to the vow he'd made Epona. It was nearing time as well for Nuri to decide her future. At Nofret's request, Nuri returned to her family for a visit the following year. She was thirteen, a graceful, lovely bud that promised the lush bloom of beauty much like her mother at that age. It was the first occasion for Mellitza and Nuri to meet. Epona had planted the seed of love long ago. The two merged as sisters of the heart. Nuri confided to her mother that she had been planning to return to Thessaloniki permanently at her fourteenth birthday. Her years of study and initiation would serve her well but she realized she wanted a family and children of her own.

"Knowing that Mellitza would journey to Philae the following year however, had changed her mind. She would extend her own training to be with Mellitza at the beginning of hers. She had already missed so many years; while they were both still young, she wanted to foster a deeper relationship. Though she had been looking forward to Nuri's return, Nofret was touched by her daughter's expression of love.

"So it came to pass that Nofret made the trip to Egypt the following year bringing Mellitza to the Temple to begin her study. They were met at the Nile landing by Nuri and Layla in a joyous reunion. While Nuri took charge of her niece, giving her a tour of the grounds, introducing her to other initiates and helping her settle into her accommodations, the women had time to spend together privately.

"Layla understood Nofret's mixed emotions at leaving both of her daughters for a separation of so many years. Gently, she soothed her tears and listened to the years of stories that had come between them since last they were together. Nuri had already told her of Mellitza's mystical birth. Nofret brought with her the sacred talisman, the caul that prophesied the gifts the child had yet to realize. She knew that it should always be near to her granddaughter.

"Layla spoke frankly, 'You know what such a birth foretells. With proper training, this child will have power beyond imagination. Such training will be exacting. We won't be easy with her simply because she is your granddaughter. You must know that, Nofret, but know too that we will cherish her. It has been a long time; we are in great need of such a one among us. I knew when I met Epona that she was special. Your son, Chenzira is fortunate. Even tho' she's gone, she exerts the mother's influence. I'm not surprised that all of this comes through you. I have a priestess who will mentor her the first few years. Her name is Muri-El; she will guide Mellitza first, into tending the bees; I heard the story already from Nuri about the bee sting on her lips. She carries such promise. You are always welcome, Nofret - you may want to spend some time with us during the years of her training. You bear great influence. What we have before us is the stuff of prophecy!'

"At that moment, the girls returned. Mellitza was already dressed in the white tunic that designated her status as initiate. She radiated innocence and excitement. Nuri would clearly be a mentor to the child as well and would ease any confusion or sadness at her departure.

"Nofret lingered a few days enjoying the visit with her dearest friend, Layla. They walked through the gardens and groves, visited the bees, spent time with Muri-El who would be first to introduce Mellitza to the careful tending of the mystical creatures. Memories of her own training flooded back. She acknowledged the choice she made in loving Aquila, how what she had learned influenced their lives together and how the enduring value of it all brought her back repeatedly over the years.

'Life is a circle indeed!' she said to Layla. 'The moment I re-enter the sanctuary of the Temple grounds my spirit and soul are embraced. I have never regretted my choice to marry. The deep refreshment I feel after a visit has only nourished and sustained me in my role as wife, mother and now grandmother. Where have the years gone?'

"Like the girls they had been, they laughed at the grey streaking their hair and the first lines circling their eyes. No reassurance was needed between them. They were women content with the choices they'd made in life.

"When Mellitza was ten and fully absorbed in her studies, Nuri decided it was finally time to return to her family. Nofret would come once again to bring her home and visit with Mellitza. Chenzira and Azad decided to accompany her on the journey. Chenzira had not been there since his wedding journey with Epona; he longed to spend time with his daughter and to meet again with Layla.

"Azad had never been to Egypt so considered the trip an opportunity to acquire goods of rare antiquity and fine craftsmanship. Over the years his business had thrived. He had an eye for beauty and was respected as a fair trade negotiator. He was a man of substance and vision.

"For all his mastery of business he was not, however, prepared for the vision of beauty he encountered on first meeting again with Nuri. He had not seen her since she left Thessaloniki when she was seven. Ten years had passed. With a twinkle in her eye that revealed the still beating gypsy heart, Nuri took his breath away. He was struck speechless. The spark between them was so tangible and profound that everyone around them was startled into stillness.

"Taking a breath, Nofret broke the spell with a gentle touch on his arm. Azad recovered his composure. Each of them present recognized silently that something of great promise had just happened. Sensitive to the awkwardness of the moment, Layla suggested that they move to their guest quarters to rest, bathe and prepare for the feast prepared in their honor. Chenzira stepped up and put his arm around his best friend. With a knowing smile and a little push, he got him moving in the right direction.

"Nuri went off in search of Mellitza who had not yet been reunited with her family. Nofret and Layla walked together acknowledging the hand of Isis in the magical binding of hearts they'd just witnessed. 'Surely our lives are entwined in mystery.' Nofret thought out loud. 'Twins came into our lives from a far country, directed on life's journey by their Great Mother and now into the holy embrace of Isis. Will wonders never cease? Blessed Be, my Sister!'

"Over the week, Mellitza proudly shared with her father so much that she was learning. He was impressed with her fearless handling of the bees. She was fascinated with their intelligence, cooperation and ability to communicate among themselves. 'You see father, it's all girl bees who do the work. They serve the Queen who serves their community all her life just like our High Priestess. There are of course some males, drones we call them. They're drawn to her by powerful pheromones and are responsible for impregnating the Queen so she can lay the eggs that will become the bees who will fly out to gather nectar and pollen that eventually they turn into honey that we will be able to draw out as liquid gold, the sweetest you've ever tasted!' Chenzira smiled, touched deeply by his daughter's excitement and knowledge.

"'This is my favorite place here in all the world! I miss you, Father, sometimes, and I'm sure you've missed me too and wondered, maybe even worried, about me from time to time. Don't ever worry! I'm young but I know I've found the purpose of my life. This whole place is sacred. I feel it in every breath I take. I hope that as time goes by, you'll visit me again but trust that I am right where I want to be.'

"Remembering the impact of their visit on the Isle of Philae so many years before, Chenzira felt himself complete in Mellitza's happiness. 'Your mother smiles upon you, sweet Mellitza. Never forget that love and her insistence that you come here when the time was right. A parent has no greater satisfaction than the contentment of their children. You are so blessed to have found yours early. Many people seek their entire lives and never find it. When our time of parting comes, you can trust that I leave with a glad heart,'

"During that same week, Nuri and Azad reclaimed the easy relationship that had been theirs in Thessaloniki though now it was charged with a fever of wondrous love. Nuri still had the spirit of gypsy in her soul, perfectly matched with Azad's energy, appreciation of beauty and even wanderlust. Since Epona's passing, Azad had not experienced such a meeting of minds. Though it had happened in the span of a breath, they recognized that their future was bound up in each other. Before they left, they asked for Layla's and Nofret's blessing.

"On the eve of their departure, the two priestesses created a lovely ritual giving thanks to Isis for the pure vision that had woven them together, imploring her to watch over them and to bless them with their hearts' desire. Such joy and amazement! Though partings are always bittersweet, all hearts were full and returned with far more than they'd ever imagined.

"Chenzira had opportunity that night to spend time with Layla. He expressed deep gratitude for Mellitza's happiness and contentment. 'You know she's special, Chenzira.' Layla spoke quietly. 'Much lies ahead for her, years of study and challenging tests to open the channels of true prophecy. She has a sense of her power already. She is a true empath, sensitive to the thoughts and feelings of those around her. With a touch, a glance or a whisper, she's able to soothe a heartache or calm a situation. Her instinctive work with the bees has furthered our understanding. I've seen them cover her body completely without a single sting, they just seem to want to taste her sweetness while she stands still delighting in their trust. I know the story of the bee sting on her lips. That too foretells her future influence. I thank the goddess for your trust in us.'

"On arriving home, Aquila was as surprised as Nofret but deeply pleased with his daughter's choice of husband. Azad was loved by everyone and their marriage was a happy one. For a while they even traveled the trade routes together satisfying the roaming curiosity of her own spirit as Azad showed her the world.

"At fourteen Mellitza made the decision that she would stay on the Isle of Philae to pursue her studies, a decision that surprised no one. Chenzira visited every few years; his daughter was his life's blessing.

"A nineteen, Mellitza was the image of the goddess. Already she was a dreamer of consequence and increasing renown. She was a healer of emotional as well as physical ailments and a much sought after midwife. She still found her greatest delight in the surround of her bees. Her honey was acclaimed as the sweetest in all of Egypt. One day while she was tending the bees she was informed that a man was at the gates seeking an audience. She sent word that he was invited to join her in the almond grove.

"His name was Amichai. He was a Jewish scholar, scribe and widower. He lived in Capernaum, on the shores of the Sea of Galilee. The death of his wife had left him without purpose or joy. Attempting to bury the pain, he'd journeyed to Egypt hoping to reclaim his life in some way. He came to Philae because his heart needed healing but also to acquire the beeswax tablets that were highly prized for their quality. Mellitza sensed his devastation at the loss of his beloved and was drawn to him like bees to the blossom. They spent the afternoon opening their hearts as he poured his out in gasping breaths. In so doing he found a modicum of relief and relaxed for the first time in years, exhausted. Under the almond trees, he fell asleep in her arms.

"In the days following, as the tablets were prepared, they fell in love. By the time his smile returned, though she told him she would not leave the island to be his wife, they drank each other's nectar in a passion neither had ever known.

"With the breath of the goddess upon them both, Mellitza recognized the moment of conception. Though he had respected her decision to remain a priestess of Isis, Amichai struggled with the realization that their love had resulted in a life. Children belong with their mother so in their remaining time together, he came to a place of acceptance that especially should the child be a girl, she would remain with Mellitza. She, of course, knew that the seed he'd placed in her womb would grow to be their daughter.

"The time for Amichai to return was approaching. In spite of his sadness at leaving, he had recovered the joy of his life and looked forward to resuming his work. For the time being, until the birth, he would remain in Alexandria so he could return more easily to the island. Though she would not be his wife, he loved Mellitza for the healing she had wrought and knew he could return to Capernaum in the near future to live with purpose, his soul restored.

"Sofia was born into the surround of peace, love and beauty, perfect in every way. Amichai returned in joy. He too had sensed early the gender of the baby and knowing thus he'd prepared himself to spend time again with his beloved even as his heart grew to bursting with love for his daughter. They parted in a month's time with the promise that he'd return each year at her birthday."

Sakinah stood up needing to stretch. It was so easy to be lost in her story. Mellitza was her grandmother after all; the story was as familiar now as her own breath. "How are you doing, Mary? Do you want me to continue or are you too tired for any more tonight?"

"I'm tired Nana but I'm glad to stop right here because I know now that the next symbol I want on my staff is a bee. I love my bees as much as Mellitza did and it seems like a miracle that they flew all the way from Egypt to live with us in Magdala! Can we do that now, Nana before I go to sleep so that maybe I can dream of my great, great grandmother as a young woman? I can see in my mind her body covered in a swarm of bees. What magic!" Sakinah and Hannah were charmed by Mary's enthusiasm and absorption in the story. Her excited request was easy to accommodate.

"Mary, your staff is really becoming a meaningful work of art." her mother told her. "The bees have an innate sense that guides them where they need to go to gather the sweetest nectar and pollen. I think the bee is a fitting image for a staff that will provide support as you move through life. It will remind you always of the true direction you seek."

Excitement was in the air the following morning. One more day and night on the road and they would reach their destination. Again the two Mary's walked together for a time holding the staff between them. Sakinah and

Hannah both recognized that the babe had dropped lower in her body, positioning himself for the passage into life. Walking or riding, Mary found it difficult to be comfortable. It wasn't long before she wanted to be carried again on the donkey's back. The child stayed close, skipping close at her side as if she too perceived that birth was near.

Spirits were high that night knowing that tomorrow the travelers would pass Jerusalem, their sacred city before arriving finally at Bethlehem early in the afternoon. There was music round the fire again, and dancing but Mary wanted more of the story so Hannah and she settled into the comfort of their tent to listen as Sakinah continued her spell-binding.

"As Sofia grew she loved nothing better than to spend time with her mother among the bees. With inherent sense they seemed to recognize whose child she was. They might alight on her shoulder, hand or offer a *kiss* on the cheek but they were always gentle. She had no fear.

"Over the years as Mellitza continued her work in the grove, observing and listening, she'd discovered the healing power of bee venom. It was Muri-El, her aging mentor who, after suffering a few accidental stings, questioned out loud the relief she'd experienced from the crippling of her hands. Was it her imagination or had something shifted? Trusting to Mellitza's tender care, Muri-El became a willing volunteer, for the pain of the disease long associated with aging, was nearing a crisis. Her fingers were closing like claws, the knuckles inflamed, zapping the strength of her hands so that even the smallest task was nearly unbearable.

"With Sofia close taking careful notes, Mellitza and Muri-El began a regime of bee stings. They started slowly with one or two stings every few days directly into the points of greatest discomfort. Quickly, after only a few treatments, her fingers began to relax and open. As Muri-El's tolerance to the venom grew, she noticed as well, an increasing energy and uplifted spirits along with the improvement to her hands. Mellitza became more aggressive, administering stings daily, several to each hand. By the end of a month, Muri-El was without pain, her fingers again flexible. They communicated their findings to Layla who encouraged them to continue the study by seeking other participants. What other ailments could be alleviated? In the bees, Mellitza had found her calling. She proceeded to experiment with Sofia becoming her able assistant.

"True to his word, Amichai returned to the Temple every year for Sofia's birthday. Sofia had great love for her father who delighted in expanding her talent as a scribe. Together they read the sacred words of scripture, a practice not openly encouraged among Jewish women. She loved the beauty of the Psalms and learned them by heart much to her father's surprise and joy. As she grew in understanding and beauty, Amichai fully acknowledged the wisdom of the Temple's teaching. As a Jewish man, his vision of life was magnified as he realized how much was denied his people due to the restrictions of the law placed upon women. Partaking of the Temple life each year, he came to understand how richly the blessing of enlightenment came through equality, balance and freedom of choice.

"As she neared her fourteenth birthday, Mellitza began discussing with Sofia that she might want to consider leaving the Temple with her father to experience more of the world. Muri-El and Layla soon joined the conversation. Layla had come to the Temple at seven and never left but Muri-El had been initiated after the death of her husband. Pilgrims from around the world frequented the Temple every year coming for inspiration, learning, peace and solace. Muri-El attested to a greater understanding and compassion because of her previous life, making her more capable in her role as priestess of Isis, the Great Mother. Sofia would always be welcome back should that be her ultimate choice but they all encouraged expansion.

"Amichai was beside himself with joy when Sofia decided she would return with him to Capernaum. Together they routed a journey through Egypt and Greece before returning to Galilee. Mellitza was confident in her daughter's choice though she knew how much she'd miss her. There was no looking back, such was Sofia's excitement. As the barge pulled away and the good-byes were for real, little did she know the life and love that lay ahead. She was clear however with her father, that life in Capernaum would include the bees!"

"While Sofia and her father continued to return to Egypt for visits with Mellitza every few years, when she was seventeen her life changed. Malechi was a fisherman, strong, smart, kind and prosperous. They met at the market where he was selling the day's catch. Sofia already had the reputation as a radical for she could read and write and assisted her father in his work. Nevertheless, she was fully accepted in the village because Amichai was a respected member of the community. Besides, Sofia's bees produced the sweetest honey in all of Galilee, much like her mother's in Egypt.

"It wasn't only her grace and beauty that attracted Malechi. He respected her intelligence, her unlikely career and her tender care of the bees. He was not looking for conformity in a wife. He found her stories of life as an initiate of Isis illuminating for among the Jews, their reputation as harlots was held in common as truth. He didn't find it necessary to ask but she assured him nevertheless, of her purity in body as well as mind.

"Amichai welcomed Malechi's interest in Sofia for he knew him to be a man of his word, capable, kind and fair minded. Their wedding was as grand an affair as Capernaum had ever seen. Nofret and Aquila came from Thessaloniki. Nuri and Azad surprised everyone by bringing Canan. Chenzira arrived from Egypt with Mellitza, Layla and Muri-El. All the people of Capernaum were invited.

"Nofret had not forgotten the ruby necklace worn by all the brides in the family from Behar to Epona. She surprised her granddaughter with it on the morning of the marriage. Together in joy, with all the women in attendance, Mellitza placed the ruby of eternal devotion around Sofia's neck.

"The Rabbi had never witnessed a gathering of such religious and cultural diversity. If it bothered him at all, he did not speak of it but rather welcomed them all. Over the years he had come to know Amichai well. He respected him as an observant Jew as well as a free thinker, never afraid to question. They often engaged in lively discussions on the Law. It was not surprising to him then, that his daughter should share a similar character and spirit."

Closing her eyes Sakinah paused, reflecting on the wonder of her story and how it had the power to clearly bring to mind the images of her beloved mother and father. Mary and Hannah, shared silently in the emotion of the moment.

Bringing herself back to the present, Sakinah opened her eyes and smiled. "I see your eyes are growing sleepy, my daughters. Because tomorrow is the long awaited day of our arrival, let me conclude with a little nutshell here before we retire for the night. We can pick up the story in the future but in the meantime, I suspect we'll be quite busy with Mary and Joseph. With all the prophesy surrounding his coming I'm not sure what will be required of us or when we'll get back to this."

"Sofia and Malachi had full lives in Capernaum. I was born into their loving arms two years after they married. It was Amichai who suggested returning to Egypt for a visit with Mellitza to secure her blessing on my life. Malechi had heard so much of life at the Temple that he was eager to make the visit as well. He and Mellitza had come to know each other well during her visit for the wedding; with foresight he fostered the bond that would develop between us.

"Malechi's respect for Mellitza and his love for Sofia, allowed him an open mind during the visit. He was thus comfortable with everything he experienced. Mellitza was thrilled with her role as grandmother and I adored her equally. Many happy hours were spent together often in the company of Layla and Muri-El.

"During the years since her visit to Capernaum, Mellitza had become deeply grounded in the ancient discipline of meditation. She'd often sit for days in the grove with her bees who seemed be the catalyst to a state of trance so profound that she was able to respond to questions with the compassion, justice and understanding of the Mother herself. She was truly becoming the long awaited Oracle.

"Knowing their time was brief, Sofia took every opportunity to be with her mother drinking deeply at the wellspring of her knowing. On one such occasion, Mellitza prophesized the birth of a daughter generations hence whose union with the Promised One would transform the old laws, freeing women to lives of equality. Her road would be fearsome but the eternal truths of balance and love would guide, protect and support her to fulfill such destiny.

"We anticipate this prophesy even as we keep alive the ancient stories that nourish our spirits and maintain balance within our families. Women will celebrate the freedom to choose, to be educated, to be valued as equal partners and to contribute our voices to the community at large without fear of censure or retribution.

"So, my dear ones, with such hope in our hearts, I draw tonight's story to a close. We need our rest for much yet lies ahead. Tomorrow Mary, you'll see for the first time, the sacred city of Jerusalem. Though we won't enter her gates this trip, you will feel her magnitude of spirit. In the afternoon Joseph will seek lodging in Bethlehem and if I am not mistaken, the birth of Jesus will take place well before we set our steps again towards home. Sleep soundly dear ones. May the angels watch over us all this night." Mary went to her grandmother and hugged her tightly. Then snuggling close to her mother's warmth, she quickly fell asleep.

Many of the travelers were up before dawn anticipating their arrival in Bethlehem. Spirits were high. Excited voices filled the air. By the day's first light, camp was packed and they were on the road again. When the sun was near its peak, Jerusalem was in sight. Taking advantage of their proximity, they paused there for refreshment, absorbing the breath of the city they considered their spiritual home.

By late afternoon they arrived in Bethlehem. The city felt chaotic after days on the open road. Bethlehem wasn't prepared for the great swell of travelers in need of accommodations. Animals, wagons and families clogged the streets and inns making it difficult to find lodging anywhere.

Urgently scouting what might be available, Joseph at last found safe haven for them in a farmer's cave nearby to the city. Upon discovering the late stage of Mary's pregnancy, the kindness of the owner and his wife afforded them beds of clean straw, light, water and nourishment. Relieved and grateful, Hannah was quick to offer one of her goatskins of mead to the farmer, bringing the hint of a smile to Joseph's weary face. The warmth given off by the animals and their gentle lowing calmed everyone's exhausted nerves. Mary and Joseph settled down to rest as Sakinah and Hannah made final preparations for the imminent birth. With all in readiness, they too, with Mary, took advantage of the quiet and fell asleep.

In the stillness of that very night, Mary began her labor. Over the next hours, a vibrational silence descended upon the circle of family as Mary labored through the night. The birth was not difficult for one so young and strong but it was her first and as such proceeded slowly. Sakinah encouraged Mary with Hannah close by.

Mary found purpose responding to their requests. Early on, Joseph realized his wife was in the best hands possible and that for the time being at least, his place was not at her side. Wrapping his cloak tightly around him, he ventured outside to walk in prayer under the stars. Hannah sent Mary out to walk with him several times over the course of the night. He welcomed her presence.

With a sensitivity born of experience attending labors beyond number, they became increasingly aware that this birth was like no other. Mary, though young, expressed no fear. She uttered no sound. Her breathing was even and deep. Though she responded easily to every signal and suggestion, she was attuned internally as if in meditation. A glow emanated from her body, its light softly illuminating their surroundings.

"And she gave birth to her firstborn son and wrapped him in bands of cloth, and laid him in a manger." (Luke 2:7)

The birth foretold through the ages had been accomplished. Mary went out into the night, drawing

Joseph back inside at last. Hannah handed the infant to Joseph. Overjoyed, he spoke from his heart in silent communion with his son. When Mary was made comfortable, Joseph handed the baby to his wife who took him eagerly to her breast.

Seeing the child Mary watching in awe near the animals, Joseph called her to them. The sound of wings and heavenly voices filled the air. Tears filled her eyes as she entered the circle of light that glowed all around them. In a loving gesture that astonished Hannah, Mary offered the infant to the child to hold. All breath stopped in the awesome sweetness of the moment.

Feeling a child's arms around him, the newborn Jesus opened his eyes. They looked into each other's souls in instantaneous recognition and surrender. A palpable current of energy wove round about them as Mary's tears fell upon his face. In a voice brimming with innocent wonder, Mary looked up exclaiming, "Oh, Mama, Nana, sweet Mary and Joseph! My heart spills over with love more than words can say. I know now my purpose in life. I know why I was born. I am his! Together we will ignite the spark of Holy Spirit!"

"Then an angel of the Lord stood before them and the glory of the Lord shone around them, and they were terrified. And suddenly there was with the angel a multitude of the heavenly host, praising God and saying: Glory to God in the highest heaven; and on earth peace among those whom he favors." (Luke 2: 9, 13, 14)

Shaken by the conviction of her daughter's words, Hannah allowed the moment to pass, absorbing the unspoken significance of such a declaration. Joseph gently took the baby from the child's arms and placed him back with his mother. At Sakinah's signal, mother and daughter retreated to the shadows. Mary came to them disoriented, tears still falling. Hannah held her trembling body close, encouraging her to breathe deeply to restore her equilibrium. Relaxing finally in her mother's arms, she fell into a peaceful slumber.

Sleep would not come so easily for the others, however. Throughout the night they were surrounded by the divine presence of angels singing. Shepherds arrived who on their watch in the hills had heard the angelic host announcing the long awaited birth. They came bearing gifts of new lambs for him who would be called king.

During the ensuing days, the child Mary engaged in all that came to pass spending many happy hours with the family. Mother Mary recovered easily, quietly sharing her unbridled joy. Adamant that she must be present for the Jewish rituals of circumcision and presentation, the child Mary insisted on staying. Soon enough they could make plans to return to Galilee.

Thus after eight days had come to pass, they all traveled to Jerusalem to present the baby Jesus in the Temple. Politely making themselves scarce while the family's religious formalities were taking place, Mary, Sakinah and Hannah were yet close enough to witness the meeting with Simeon. Blessing the young mother, Simeon who had waited all his life for this moment, took the babe into his arms and said, *"This child is destined for the falling and the rising of many in Israel, and to be a sign that will be opposed so that the inner thoughts of many will be* revealed – and a sword will pierce your own soul too." (Luke 2: 34-35)

At that same moment, Anna, the ancient prophetess who lived in the Temple, stepped forward to offer her blessing.

She *"began to praise God and to speak about the child to all who were looking for the redemption of Jerusalem"* (Luke 2:38).

Startled and afraid upon hearing such predictions, Mary leaned into and nearly collapsed against Joseph. Gathering together, the group left the Temple in stunned silence hurriedly returning to their lodging. Hannah and Sakinah, grateful they had lingered with the family after all, helped to settle nerves with calming tea and the quiet assurance of their gentle ministrations.

With a child's simple innocence, Mary suggested prayer to find a blessing in the present moment. Throughout the confusion, she had provided the warmth of a steady handhold to Jesus' mother. As all hands lifted to hearts in prayer, little Mary had to shake hers back into circulation. Without even realizing, Mary's unrelenting grip of fear had put the child's hand to sleep. Tensions eased and tentative smiles returned as Mary shook life, breath and blood back, not only into her little hands but into hearts struggling to understand. Finally joining in prayer, grace descended upon them and peace prevailed.

Restored in faith, it came to pass that they received a visit from three magnificent Magi. Following a star out of the east, they came first to the court of King Herod where they sought directions. Herod knew nothing of such a birth but requested that once the royal babe was located, they should return to him with news of how to find him, for he too wanted to pay homage. The wise men came at last to the dwelling of the family, honoring the infant whose birth had long been prophesized. They arrived bearing gifts of frankincense, gold, and myrrh.

In a dream, an angel warned the Magi not to return to Herod for he was no more than jealous despot. In truth, no tribute would *he* pay to a *king* of the Jews!

Joseph too was warned by the angel who ordered him to prepare his family and hasten to the land of Egypt. Herod, angry that the three had not returned as commanded, made plans to send his soldiers in search of the child. To assure his destruction, the troops would be dispatched with orders to kill all male children under the age of two.

In the morning, Joseph shared his dream with the others. Sakinah, Hannah and his wife listened anxiously.

The child was first to speak. "Joseph, Mary! I am to travel with you! Herod's soldiers will be looking for a couple with only a wee babe not a girl child my size. Jesus will be easy to hide. During this entire journey, Nana, you've talked of purpose and trust, balance and choice. I know I am here to protect Jesus and to love him all my life." Looking directly into her mother's eyes, Mary spoke gently but firmly, "Jesus needs me now more than you do, Mama. When danger subsides, I'll return home. In the meantime, I have my staff to support me with its bee to guide me true."

Joseph listened intently, stilled to consideration by the assurance in her voice and the common sense of her suggestion. Sakinah and Hannah looked at each other as Mellitza's prophecy rose before them.

Sakinah spoke with urgency. "Do you know where in Egypt you will go, Joseph?"

"I will trust the angel of the Lord to direct us," he answered.

"Mary's idea carries more value than you know, Joseph." Sakinah attested. "She's young but she too has a mission that has been foretold. My grandmother Mellitza, is High Priestess in Egypt at the Temple of Isis on the Isle of Philae. She would not only take you in, she would hide you safely until such time that you can return to Nazareth.

"Mellitza is the Oracle of Isis. Decades ago she proclaimed that a daughter would be born into our family who in union with her twin flame, will bring equality, forgiveness and justice in a new law based on love. Herod's evil is far reaching, even beyond the borders of his own country. He would never think to search for a family of Jews in the Temple of Isis. It's a perfect plan."

Joseph laid aside his initial skepticism and conceded. "As I have trusted you and Hannah with the very lives of my wife and son; as I have come to love the child Mary, I will trust that it is the angel of the Lord who has entwined our lives in this manner and who now directs us to this island of protection."

Finding agreement in his wife's eyes, he turned to Mary's mother. "What say you, Hannah? Does this plan suit you? Will you be able to depart for home without your blessed daughter at your side? What will your husband say when you return without her?"

"Joseph, I too was trained on Philae with my great grandmother. She is as wise and loving as your own wife Mary and her mother Anna. I'll miss my Mary of course, but I know it's not forever and that she will be safe with you until then. Mellitza is ancient but as this journey has evolved, I now know that she has been awaiting this birth and your arrival for years.

"As for my husband Ari, he honors me with his trust and will respect my decision. We will miss her to be sure but life moves quickly. Before you know it, you'll be back in Nazareth and Mary will be back with us in Magdala. Perhaps that will happen even before the birth of the child I now carry in my womb."

All eyes turned abruptly to Hannah, anxiety turning to smiles. "Mama! You're going to have a baby too!"

Sakinah gazed lovingly at her daughter. "You didn't tell me! Does Ari know?"

"It was confirmed over the course of our journey. I didn't tell Ari before we left, I wanted to be sure. This is no replacement for you sweet Mary, but it will make our empty nest more bearable for your papa and me until you return."

"It's settled then." said Joseph. "We are deeply grateful to you both in so many ways. The arrival of this One has many ramifications. We are humbled to be chosen as his parents and will raise him with hearts open to the sacred and timeless voice of love, knowing now that it may be heard through unexpected channels."

While Joseph was gone to make arrangements for a horse and cart, Mary spoke quietly with Sakinah and Hannah. "Mother, as the angel came to Joseph in the night, I was visited by Mellitza as I slept. It was she who planted the seed of this plan; she assures me of its safety. Herod indeed wants to destroy this babe. It's urgent that we all leave as quickly as possible. Have no fear, she told me. She is aware of the prophecy and assured me of our safety on the road ahead."

Listening intently to the child's dream, Mary stood and walked over to them clasping the baby Jesus to her breast. As their arms encircled each other instinctively, they were surrounded in a column of vibrational light. Words escaped them all. Looking deeply into each other's very souls, they found the confidence and courage needed to move forward.

The farmer's wife entered their lodging just as Joseph returned. She brought food, water and extra blankets for the journey. Hannah stepped forward quietly to whisper to the young mother, "Mary, please take with you these two tiny vials of precious Royal Jelly. Know that *all* the forces of heaven travel with you and that you will arrive safely at your destination. Please give one of them to Mellitza in gratitude, for it was she who taught us how to love and care for our bees. The other, directly from my sweet queen, is for your little prince. May you go in peace and return to us swiftly when the time is right!" With one last warm embrace and swift kisses on the cheek, they turned their attention to their final departure.

Joseph came in from hitching the horse to the wagon and quickly loaded their few supplies. Little Mary brought only some change of clothing and her precious walking staff. Joseph insisted that Hannah and Sakinah take the donkey for the journey back to Magdala. Fortuitously, a caravan was leaving that morning traveling back to Galilee. There was time only to get underway.

With quick hugs and more than a few tears, they said their goodbyes. The little group including the farmer and his wife watched as the cart rumbled away down the dusty road. As Sakinah and Hannah lifted their arms in a final blessing of farewell, round about them was heard a mounting crescendo of sound that seemed to come from nowhere and everywhere. Its intensity grew as if alive. Looking up to the sky to identify the source of such ethereal power, swarms of bees were seen coming from all directions. Even the sun was over-shadowed as the waves of winged creatures beyond number joined forces. As the cart and horse with its precious cargo, moved off into the far distance, the swarms circled around them then lifted high above. It appeared that a certain band moved into the lead directing the others into instinctive formation; a heavenly escort of divine protection guiding them safely upon their road to destiny.

Epilogue

Trusting the wisdom of ancient prophesy
they each went their own way
passing into the pages of history,
the Bible, myth and religion.
Imagined, maligned, condemned and forgiven,
Mary became the stuff of legend.
Thorn in the side of Peter the Rock
... yet ...
Apostle to the Apostles
Beloved of Jesus
Reformer and Visionary
Equal Partner
in the eternal message of truth He came to deliver -
Grace, Love, Forgiveness, Peace of the Holy Spirit.

Mary's mission continues to inspire
exhorting us to seek our own truth and purpose
May this story continue for each of you
according to your own heart.

Afterword

As so much of history and Bible study are open to speculation, the opportunity and challenge belong to each of us to read between the lines, seeking the truth and fullness of the story.

Just as her mother and grandmothers went off to the Temple at the age of seven, the child Mary, at the age of seven, is guided in a dream to lead the way into Egypt.

Called by the Ancient One, her Great-Great Grandmother Mellitza, Mary responds fearlessly, without hesitation, embarking upon the path of her destiny. She carries only her cherished walking staff; a creation that will continue to provide support and sweet succor as she walks the many roads of her life.

Trusting the wisdom of Mellitza's long-ago prophecy, Sakinah and Hannah present no objection to Mary's decision. Sakinah's stories after all, were intended to encourage self-reliance and bold choices. Hannah and Sakinah know the child is in good hands, protected by the common bond and love of both Mary and Joseph.

On the brink of the age of reason, Mary has only begun to awaken to the realization of her intertwined relationship with Jesus and the divine mission they are to share.

Historically, after a time in Egypt, Mary, Joseph and Jesus return to Nazareth. Will Mary return with them or will she stay on the Isle of Philae through initiation and training, absorbing as much as possible from Mellitza while she still lives? What sacred teachings might prepare her for the ecstatic love she will experience and the dark night of the soul she will encounter in the years ahead? Could Mary learn to confront life's demons by developing the impenetrable defense of illuminated chakras, raising her power through their pure vibration into a state of union with the divine? Is it possible that even Jesus returns later to the Temple for an initiation of his own, incorporating *all* facets of Holy Woman Spirit into his future ministry? How will the special bond between the two Marys ripen over time?

I don't know the answers either. I don't even know all the questions! This, so far, is the story given to me. While the writing of Mary's journey flowed easily, I find myself baffled when it comes to knowing Jesus. Any acknowledgment of a divine feminine is missing from all the stories. I hunger for the nourishment to be found in the sweet *"... honey of the rock."* (Psalm 81: 16) the soul food intimated by a bountiful Mother Father God. Might Mary's evolving story open a deeper understanding of the esoteric depth and meaning of the man called Jesus? Perhaps, the journey has just begun.

The Last Word

This story would not be complete without acknowledging
the powerful influence of the bees.
My dear husband has been a faithful steward
of these mystical creatures for years.
I sit with them often seeking, in some small way,
to honor their devotion and vital importance to humankind.
They came naturally into this story.
How grateful I am to have caught their buzz!

Selected Bibliography

New Revised Standard Version Bible, 1989

Campbell, Joseph, *The Power of Myth,* Anchor Books 1991

Diamont, Anita, *The Red Tent,* Picador 1997

Forth, Sarah S., Ph.D. *Eve's Bible,* St. Martin's Press, 2008

George, Margaret, *Mary Called Magdalene,* Penguin Books, 2002

Gimbutas, Marija, *Civilization of the Goddess,* Harper San Francisco 1991

Heartsong, Claire, *Anna, Grandmother of Jesus,* S.E.E. Publishing 2002

Leloup, Jean-Yves, *The Gospel of Mary Magdalene,* Inner Traditions, 2002

Napoli, Donna Jo, *Song of the Magdalene,* Simon Pulse, 2004

Shelby Spong, John, *Born of a Woman, A Bishop Rethinks the Birth of Jesus,* Harper San Francisco 1992

Starbird, Margaret, *The Woman with the Alabaster Jar,* Bear & Co. 1993

Stone, Merlin, *When God Was a Woman,* A Harvest/HBJ Book, 1978

Walker, Barbara, *Woman's Encyclopedia of Myths and Secrets,* Harper & Row 1983

Characters

Alon married Freyda; daughter of Norman; father of Canan

Amichai: Jewish scholar, beloved of Mellitza, Priestess of Isis; father of Sofia

Aquila (Roman) married Nofret (Egyptian); parents of Chenzira and Nuri

Ari: husband of Hannah and father of Mary Magdalene, son-in-law of Sakinah

Azad: son of Canan and Alon; Epona's twin brother; married Nuri, daughter of Nofret and Aquila

Baruch: husband of Sakinah, father of Hannah, deceased grandfather of Mary Magdalene

Behar: visionary of her people; married Norman; step-mother of Freyda

Canan: daughter of Alon and Freyda; married Karim; mother of twins Epona and Azad, grandmother of Mellitza and Valens

Chenzira: son of Aquila and Nofret; married Epona; father of Valens and Mellitza

Epona: daughter of Alon and Canan; Azad's twin sister; married Chenzira; mother of Valens and Mellitza

Freyda: daughter of Norman; step-daughter of Behar; married Alon; mother of Canan; grandmother to the twins – Epona and Azad

Hannah: daughter of Sakinah; wife of Ari; mother of Mary Magdalene

Karim: husband of Canan; father of twins Epona and Azad

Layla: High Priestess of Isis

Malachi married Sofia, daughter of Amichai and Mellitza

Mary Magdalene: daughter of Hannah and Ari, granddaughter of Sakinah; great-granddaughter of Sofia

Mellitza: daughter of Epona and Chenzira; beloved of Amichai; mother of Sofia; Great-Great Grandmother of Mary Magdalene; High Priestess and Oracle of Isis

Muri-El: Priestess of Isis and mentor of Mellitza

Nofret: Priestess of Isis, wife of Aquila, mother of Chenzira and Nuri, grandmother of Valens and Mellitza

Norman: widower from the north; Freyda's father, married Behar

Nuri: daughter of Aquila and Nofret; married Azad

Sakinah: married Baruch; mother of Hannah; grandmother of Mary Magdalene, storyteller

Sofia: daughter of Mellitza and Amichai; married Malachi; mother of Sakinah; Great Grandmother of Mary Magdalene

Valens: son of Epona and Chenzira, brother of Mellitza

About the Author

The uncompromising religion of childhood led Joan to discover the ancient feminine. A restless heart continues to seek balance in life's divine mystery. With husband, dog, and honeybees, she lives in Michigan's north woods—an artist, grandmother, and yoga teacher. Her first book, *This Garden Grows a Goddess*, was published in 2005.

CPSIA information can be obtained
at www.ICGtesting.com
Printed in the USA
FFOW02n1652010516
23685FF